The Laura Line

Also by Crystal Allen

HOW LAMAR'S BAD PRANK
WON A BUBBA-SIZED TROPHY

The Laura Line

Crystal Allen

BALZER + BRAY
An Imprint of HarperCollins*Publishers*

Balzer + Bray is an imprint of HarperCollins Publishers.

The Laura Line

www.harpercollinschildrens.com

Library of Congress Cataloging-in-Publication Data

Allen, Crystal.

The Laura Line / Crystal Allen. — 1st ed.

p. cm.

Summary: When Laura Dyson's seventh grade history teacher schedules a class trip to the slave shack on her grandmother's farm, Laura is forced to come to terms with her family's past and what it means for her future.

ISBN 978-0-06-199274-2 (hardcover bdg.)

[1. Schools—Fiction. 2. Self-perception—Fiction. 3. Popularity—Fiction. 4. Grandmothers—Fiction. 5. African Americans—Fiction. 6. Overweight persons—Fiction. 7. Slavery—Fiction.] I. Title.

PZ7.A42527Lau 2013 2012022165
[Fic]—dc23 CIP
AC

Typography by Carla Weise

13 14 15 16 17 CG/RRDH 10 9 8 7 6 5 4 3 2 1

❖

First Edition

To my mother, Thelma Ann Jones,
and the multitude of strong women in my line.
Because of you, I know I can do anything.

chapter one

Sweet Mother of *Teen Vogue* magazine, I'm model-marvelous in this new outfit! And when the doors of the bus open like stage curtains, I pooch my lips, raise my chin, and use the school sidewalk as my runway. A rhythm I didn't know I had moves my feet to a beat only I can hear. But it's all good because *I know* I look amazing.

This shiny black-and-gray sweater with the matching black pants is getting lots of looks from my classmates. That's because this outfit screams, "Laura Dyson's in the house!" and I'm going to let it talk for me all day.

My girl Sage will be here soon, so I lean against a pole and cop a pose while I wait for her bus. The spring breeze blows my pigtails, and I can't help but think the wind is just trying to cool me down because I look so hot. I close my eyes and daydream as my thoughts quickly drift to an exotic island in the Caribbean, where a photographer gives me detailed instructions on how to pose for the cover of *Girls' Life*. I've got my outfit *and* my attitude working the cameras as the entire crew gives me thumbs-ups and huge smiles.

But suddenly the smiles turn upside down. And so do the thumbs as my daydream fades.

"Hey, Fat Larda! Hahahaha!"

The exotic island disappears when the laughter grows louder. My eyelids snap open, and there, in front of me, is a giggly crowd of my classmates, led by Sunny Rasmussen. Sunny scans my outfit, rolls her eyes, and says the worst thing ever.

"Are you daydreaming again or just holding up the pole behind you, Fat Larda?"

I step away from the pole and squint. "The name's Laura."

She smirks and passes me. "That was almost as funny as the costume you're wearing."

I study my outfit. Am I wearing a costume? Was I wrong? Heck to the double no! This outfit bangs. I've figured out Sunny's problem. She's mad because today, I'm the best-dressed seventh grader in Brooks County, Texas, and maybe even on the whole planet.

If I were a student in a modeling academy instead of here, I wouldn't have to deal with haters like Sunny Rasmussen. I'd learn about fashion and makeup and cool stuff like that instead of the useless junk I'm taught here at Royal Middle School. Why do I need an English class? Models don't talk, they walk. And I don't need math. It's not about how many steps I take, it's about how smoothly I stroll down the runway. And the only history I'll need is what I wore yesterday so I don't wear the same thing two days in a row.

"Laura!"

It's Sage, but I can tell by the way she keeps looking left and right before stepping off the bus that something's wrong. I'm thinking her drama has to do with why she's wearing a coat buttoned all the way up to her neck. I frown, then point and wiggle my finger at her.

"Sage, what's—"

She blows by me. "Come on, I need your help."

I don't want to run, because when I do, my thighs rub together and my pants will make that *weeshy-sweeshy* noise. This outfit is supposed to be beautiful, not musical. I try to keep up with her and dig for clues at the same time. "Can you slow down a little and tell me what's wrong?"

She yanks the school door and it flies wide open as she heads down the hall toward the girls' restroom near the back of the building. Nobody uses that restroom because the Dumpster is near it and sometimes it reeks in there. But this spot is perfect for us because we don't have to worry about other girls watching us or asking us what size we wear.

"Just hurry, Laura."

"Okay, okay, I'm right behind you."

In the restroom, Sage slides her backpack down her arms until it plops on the tile near her feet. She unbuttons her coat, peels it off, and lets it drop on the floor, too. She's wearing the new outfit she bought last night. I can't help but grin as she slowly spins in front of me.

"Be honest, Laura. Does this make me look . . . you know?"

Sage is always looking for something to make her look thinner. She never uses language like "fat" or "big" to describe her shape. Anything she's uncomfortable saying, she just won't, as if the words were forbidden.

I shake my head. "You look great, Sage!"

She pulls at the collar of her black-and-white blouse, then fluffs her hair.

"Seriously, does the white in this blouse clash with my blond hair? It's too much black and white, isn't it?

What about up front? Does it hide my . . . you know?"

I examine her from head to toe, even walk around her. She moves one of my pigtails off the front of my shoulder to the back and grins at me.

"By the way, you look fabulous. And I like your necklace."

I touch my necklace and freeze. That's it! I back up toward the mirror, rest my backpack on the sink, unzip it, and dig deep in the corner, near my candy stash. There it is! I keep a vinyl pouch with extra jewelry, just in case I don't have time to put it on before I leave home. I reach inside the pouch and grab two red bracelets, red earrings, and the matching red necklace. I hand Sage the bracelets and earrings.

"Here, Sage, put these on while I fasten your necklace."

Sage shoves her hand through the bracelets until they loop her wrists, and then puts the earrings on. She looks my way. I grin with my hands on my hips.

"We look gorgeous!" I turn her toward the mirror. "See for yourself."

Sage stares at her reflection. Her eyebrows lower as she vogues with me. Then she reaches over and gives me a hug.

"You are such a fashion goddess, Laura! The red sets off this outfit in the best way ever."

I zip my jewelry pouch as Sage pulls a brush from

her coat pocket. She brushes her long hair and talks at the same time.

"Did you get your essay done last night?"

I nod. "Yeah. It was a hard choice between being a model and . . ."

She stops brushing. "Don't say it, Laura. . . ."

". . . a baseball pitcher."

She's glaring at me. "Sooooo, you wrote your essay on . . ."

I stare at the sink. "Why I want to be a model when I get out of college."

Sage sighs. "Good. Baseball's not a girl thing, Laura. How many woman pitchers are there in the major leagues? Let's see . . . how about none!"

I hold up a finger. "That's not true. There's women pitchers in the minor leagues and one even threw batting practice in Arizona during spring training."

Sage sighs. "Okay. How many girls here in *Brooks County* play baseball? Zip. Zero. None-zo Rapunzo! Stick with modeling. It's safer. You won't get laughed at."

I think about Sunny. "Yeah, maybe you're right."

I keep digging through my backpack but quickly stop. "Oh, no."

Sage steps closer. "What are you looking for?"

"I think I left my calculator at home."

The restroom is so quiet that we can hear voices through the air-conditioner vent. Sage puts her brush down. "Mr. Belcher hasn't done a supplies check in fifth period this week."

I shake my head. "Third period either."

I'm in deep trouble, and Sage says what I already know.

"Then today's the day. You're gonna get a zero if you don't have that calculator."

The first bell rings, and that means classes start in five minutes. I dig like crazy in my bag. "I've got to find it! I can't get a zero for the day, not over a dumb calculator!"

Sage opens her backpack and hands me hers. "Here. Problem solved."

I take the calculator and breathe a sigh of relief. "Thanks, Sage."

She grins, and puts her hand on my shoulder. "I will always . . ."

I nod and put my hand on hers. ". . . have your back."

We flick imaginary dust off each other's shoulders, gather our things, and rush to class.

I make it to English just before the bell rings. Once I place my essay with the others on Mr. Helms's desk, I take my seat in the back of the first row. I like it there because I can rest my shoulders on the cement wall when it gets too hot in class, and that helps me cool down.

Mr. Helms steps in, closes the door, and takes attendance. Then he grabs the stack of reports.

"Well, this stack feels pretty good. I'm guessing each of you got your essay finished. Let's have some fun. I'll read a few titles and you try to guess the writer, okay?"

Mr. Helms mixes the reports up as if he's shuffling cards, then pulls one from the stack.

"This one is entitled, 'Why I Want to Be a Professional Baseball Player.' Any guesses?"

Hands go up everywhere. Mr. Helms calls on Jake Collins.

"That's got to be Shane Doyles's essay."

Mr. Helms smiles. "You're right! Here's another. 'Why I Want to Be a Pediatrician.'"

Everybody knows that's Bindu Shah's. Both of her parents are pediatricians. Somebody shouts out the answer, and Mr. Helms puts his hand up.

"Let's keep it fair. Please raise your hand instead of shouting out the answer. Okay, this next one is entitled, 'Why I Want to Be a Professional Model.' Any guesses?"

I look around the room, wondering if anyone else has the same dream I've got. Mr. Helms calls on five different students and they all give wrong answers. He stands at my desk.

"The correct answer is Laura Dyson."

First there's silence, and I'm thinking I've blown

everybody away. But then whispers turn to giggles that explode into full-blown laughter. Heat rushes through my chest and up my neck, filling my head, because they're not just laughing at me right now, they're laughing at me in the future, too. Shane Doyles laughs louder than anyone as he adds my nickname to his chuckle.

"Fat Larda."

Mr. Helms snaps a response. "Shane, one more remark like that and you're out of here!"

Now everybody's staring at me as if I'm the one who got Shane in trouble. I grab the ends of my pigtails and stare at my desk. I hate this class.

Once the room's quiet again, Mr. Helms reads the title of the next essay. Hands go up in the air as my classmates correctly guess the writer. I tune out the guessing game and realize Sage was wrong. I could've written about baseball because it didn't matter. They were going to laugh at me no matter what I wrote.

chapter two

By third period my new strut has faded back into my old shuffle. It didn't take long for my essay title to get around school. In between classes, I get the same question. "Is it true that you want to be a professional model?"

I hold my head up. "Yes, it's true."

"Hahahahaha!"

By fourth period I'm ready to go home. Other than Sage, nobody's complimented my outfit, and the only thing being whispered about me is that I've made a bad career choice.

On my way to lunch, I find Sage standing near the

cafeteria door with an old-timey town-crier bell, selling copies of the school newspaper.

"Get your *Royal Crier* here for just a quarter. It's loaded with the latest news and gossip." She flips her hair over her shoulders and hands me a free one. I take it without looking at her.

Sage whispers, "Are you okay, Laura?"

I ignore the question and stare at the newspaper, hoping she won't ask about the essay. Just to be sure, I switch the conversation to her photography skills. "You're golden with a camera. This front-page picture bangs."

She blushes. "Thanks. Save me a seat, okay?"

I nod. "Don't I always?"

Sage and I have been best friends since third grade. That was when we realized how much bigger we were than the other kids in our class. It didn't really bother us until our classmates realized it, too. Then one day, during recess, Sage and I got corralled like cattle. We thought it was a new game until I listened to what they were shouting at us.

"Fat Larda, big as a Honda! Submarine Sage lives in an underwater cage!"

I broke through the circle, but Sage stayed, crying. So I went back in, took her hand, and pulled her out of that crowd.

"Let's go! We don't need them!"

Sage kept looking back. "But they're our friends!"

I refused to let go until we were far away from them. "No they're not! Not anymore!"

She cried harder. I turned, hugged her, and whispered in her ear. "Don't cry. I will always have your back. We'll start our own group of friends."

But our new group never grew beyond Sage and me. So we did everything together, and after all these years, we still do. I can't help but wonder what it would've been like to have more friends to hang out with and do fun things like slumber parties, walking the mall, going to the movies, and other stuff girl crews do. And the way Sage tries so hard to make a good impression, I know she wishes we had a bigger group, too.

I've made it to the daily lunch specials area, but I pass right by it. I'm almost at the end of the food selections and my tray's still empty. Someone says, "I bet Larda snatches five chocolate puddings and three milks for lunch." I turn around, but no one's looking my way. So I push my tray past the pudding, past the cold sandwiches; and just before the line ends, I spot what I want.

Sitting on crushed ice is a black plastic bowl of lettuce with one cucumber slice and three carrot threads. If I'm lucky, I'll find a tomato hidden somewhere in the mix. Taped to the cling wrap on top of the bowl is a packet of see-through dressing. I put the bowl on my tray.

When I pull a bottled water out of the ice, there

are whispers about my healthy choices. I grin to myself because it's all part of the game I play in the cafeteria. I make sure the only thing anybody sees me eat in here is a pile of raw veggies. It's easier that way, and everybody goes home happy. My delicious snacks are hidden in the backpack.

I have to be slick with snacks, because if anyone catches me chewing on an Almond Joy, they'll start those Larda jokes again, and I'm not trying to hear that.

Sage's voice rings in the cafeteria. "Laura, grab me a salad, too!"

I get her the same lunch I'm having and rest my tray across the table she saved for us. I take a seat, then wipe the mist from my forehead.

"We were so right about Belcher. He did a supplies check this morning. Thanks. Here's your math stuff back."

I place the salad, water, and calculator in front of her. Sage starts on her salad.

"I'm so glad it's Friday. And my English teacher complimented me on my outfit. I was thinking about going back to the mall and getting a pair of shoes to match, because . . ."

She trails off as most of the chatter in the cafeteria dies. I look around to see what caused Sage to shut down and spot three skinny girls at the cafeteria entrance, all dressed in pink.

I find the tomato in my salad and stab it. "Here we go. Time for the Pink Chip parade."

Sunny Rasmussen, London Miles, and Amanda Kerns sashay around the tables like they're from Planet Superior. Sunny leads the pack, and she's heading our way. When they stop at our table, Sage freezes with her fork halfway between her bowl and her mouth. Sunny ignores me, holds up a copy of the *Royal Crier,* and eyeballs my friend.

"Your name is Sage, right?"

Sage looks left, then right, and over both shoulders. "Me? Yeah, Sage, that's right."

Sunny drops the newspaper on the table. "You took this picture, didn't you?"

Sage nods, and I stop eating in case she needs my help. But Sunny cracks a devilish grin.

"I like how you got the Pink Chips in it. Are you the only photographer for the *Crier*?"

Sage doesn't blink. "Uh-huh."

Sunny picks up the newspaper. "Perfect. I've got a few ideas. Let's talk later?" She turns to face London and Amanda, then says one word. "Leaving."

Without waiting for Sage's response, the Pink Chips move on. I tap my fork on the side of my bowl. "They're gone. You can act normal now."

Sage blinks a hundred times, as if coming out of a trance, then pushes her salad away.

"Sunny knows my name. She said we'll talk later. I wonder what she wants."

I shrug. "I'm sure it has everything to do with your camera skills."

I take a swig of water and notice Sage is lost in space again. I shake her arm.

"Hey! Do you need a reboot? Stop acting like a frozen computer!"

Sage's eyes zero in on mine. "Sunny spoke to me! This is major!"

I shrug again because I don't know what else to do. "Congratulations, I guess. I know how much you want to hang out with them."

Sage returns to earth with a grin. "Don't hate."

I giggle and scoot back. "I'm finished with this salad. It's horrible. If I don't see you after school, I'll try to call you tonight. But remember, it's a major weekend at my house."

Sage stabs her fork into the last few pieces of lettuce in my bowl. "I was going to talk to you about that before the Pink Chips walked up. Is your aunt Carmen still coming in tonight?"

I smile and pick up my tray. "Yeah. I'm excited! Anyway, talk with you later."

I walk out of the cafeteria and lose the smile I gave to Sage. I love Aunt Carmen, but my parents haven't even left yet, and I already miss them.

chapter three

After lunch, I head to the office, since I'm the helper during fifth period. Mrs. Wallace, our principal's assistant, smiles on her way to the fax machine. "Your mom's been faxing stuff to us all day about leaving for military duty and emergency contact information. Does she still teach science at the community college?"

I nod and look out the window.

This Sunday afternoon, my parents leave for Killeen, Texas. They're in the Army Reserve and got official papers to report for training exercises at Fort Hood. They'll be gone two whole weeks, and

Killeen is a long drive from here.

I take in a big breath of office air, then slowly give it back. Even though I'm bummed, I can't help but think about last night at the dinner table, when Dad tossed me a baseball ticket. I thought it was for another college game. But I was wrong.

"The Houston Astros? Are you taking me to the season opener on Sunday?"

He winked. "Kind of a going-away gift from me and your mom."

Remembering that makes me smile, and when the bell rings, I snap out of my daydream and leave the front office. History is my last class of the day, but I've got my reasons for being early. Even though the late bell won't ring for another three minutes, I'm already seated and watching the door. There's no one else in the room right now, and that's how I like it. But any minute, that's going to change.

While I wait, I reach inside my backpack and unwrap a mini Almond Joy so when I'm ready for a snack, the crackly paper won't get me busted. Do I have time to check my lip gloss?

Uh-oh. I don't. There he is.

I tug at my blouse to make sure it hasn't risen on me and crack a smile.

"Hey, Troy."

He nods but doesn't look my way. "Hey."

Just the sound of his voice makes me squirm, as if I didn't know I wasn't comfortable until he spoke to me. Sweet Mother of Milk Chocolate Hunky Chunkies, that boy is ultra fine. And he's sportin' dimples shaped like half-moons, deep enough for me to climb inside and ride all the way to the mall! He's the *only* reason I'm early to history class, because when it comes to looking at Troy, there's no difference between him and my cell phone: I want all my minutes.

Soon, the late bell rings just as Sunny rushes in and takes her seat next to Troy. Mrs. Jacobs walks in and closes the door. With Sunny in the way, I no longer have a clear view of my hunky chunky. So I ease my bottom to the left until I only have one butt cheek on the chair. Now, if I lean to the right, move my head just a little, slump, and rotate . . . wait . . . there he is. I'm all twisted up, but I don't care. As I fidget, my stomach makes funny but familiar noises.

Goink . . . gurgle . . . oygoygoy.

It's like a built-in alarm clock. Even though I just had lunch two periods ago, when my belly bell goes off, it can only mean one thing—snack time. I straighten up and scan the room just to see how close Mrs. Jacobs is to my desk. She's walking and talking about slaves and that slave ship called the *Amistad.* But my classmates are texting, passing notes, or already asleep.

Wait. That's perfect! No one's paying attention! I

reach into my open backpack, slide a piece of already-unwrapped Almond Joy between my lips, and take the tiniest, ladylike bite like I've seen those models do. Mmmm.

My eyelids slowly close as the coconut and chocolate melt down the sides of my tongue like lava from a sugar volcano. Suddenly, Mrs. Jacobs holds up a stack of handouts.

"Take one and pass the rest to the person behind you, *por favor*."

Even though this is history class, I like it when Mrs. Jacobs mixes things up and speaks Spanish. Just being in her class has taught me a few Spanish words, like *por favor* means "please" and *gracias* means "thank you" and *magnifico* means "magnificent" or "awesome."

I take the handout and count three pages. On the first page, there are pencil drawings of human head silhouettes. They're not that good. I can't even tell if they're men or women. Mrs. Jacobs continues up and down the aisles as she talks.

"We've read about the amazing story of the *Amistad*, but here's a closer look at all thirty-six captives aboard the ship. We're not going to study them all—only four very special ones."

I wait for her to look my way, because I think we've studied this slave stuff long enough and it's time to drop the anchor on this *Amistad* ship. So when she looks my way, I slowly roll my eyes down to look at the handout and then back at her. To me, I've sent a clear message, but I wonder if Mrs. Jacobs understands the language of Look. If she does, that would make her trilingual with English, Spanish, and Eyeish. I'm glaring at her, but I guess she's not fluent, because she breaks our eye contact and flips a few pages before telling us what to do.

"Please turn to the last page and read the descriptions for captives numbered thirty-three, thirty-four, thirty-five, and thirty-six. They're all under the age of ten. I'll give you a moment and then we'll discuss them."

I flip the pages and my finger roams down to number thirty-three:

> *33. Kali: A small boy, stolen by slave traders while in the streets. He had parents, a brother, and a sister;*
>
> *34. Teme: A young girl taken by slave traders in the middle of the night. Father killed. Had not seen her mother or sisters since that night;*
>
> *35. Kagne: A little girl who was given to slave traders by her father to pay back a debt he owed; and*
>
> *36. Margru: A small girl who was sold into slavery to pay a debt.*

My brain keeps trying to shove what I just read into a "not true" folder. These four kids were under the age of ten? That means they were still in elementary school. I have to read each description twice because I keep seeing little clips of what I think happened come to life in my head. I sit very still at my desk, as if hiding like I think they tried to do.

There's crazy heat warming the inside of my stomach. I'm not hungry, and I don't feel sick. But something's definitely trying to get my attention. Maybe it's my "knower."

That's what Mom calls my internal right/wrong meter. She says my knower is something God gave to all girls. It works like a sixth sense and gets better, stronger, and smarter as we become women.

Just as I look up to see if anybody else is having a hard time with these stories, my eyes meet Mrs. Jacobs's. And for the first time, I think maybe she *does* understand Eye-ish, especially after she says what I'm thinking.

"Yes. These stories are true. Can you imagine yourself in their place?"

I grab one of my pigtails and twist the ends. My answer is heck to the tenth power of no. I would have been the worst slave ever, because it looks like hair perms and skin lotion hadn't been invented yet. That equals ashy, nappy, and unhappy all in the same day.

Plus I don't get how a whole continent of people let a ship full of wimps capture them, beat them, shackle up their hands and feet, and treat them like wild animals. Just the thought makes me mad. I know somewhere down the line, in my own ancestry, somebody went through this exact same torture as a slave.

I bet if Mrs. Jacobs asked every student in this room about their family history, most of them would claim they came from some royal bloodline like George Washington or King Henry. But what can I say? My peeps were probably owned by my classmates' ancestors. I know for a fact that some of my kinfolk were slaves, because my grandma's still got the shack they lived in sittin' on her farm.

And she treats that ugly shack like it's the White House. She's even got a flower bed in front of it. To me, that's as dumb as a cotton candy machine in a dentist's office.

Everything about slavery was ugly and awful. I bet if I went inside that shack—which I won't—and closed my eyes, I could hear the screams of my dead relatives. I can't imagine the terrible things that went on inside of that thing. And I'm mad at my family for keeping something so evil and embarrassing as a slave shack. It's like having a torture chamber on display and being proud of it.

I'm deep in family shack-shame when Mrs. Jacobs

starts babbling again. "After the *Amistad* docked in America, Kali, Teme, Kagne, and Margru were almost sold into slavery, but a tremendous act of love saved them. We'll talk more about that later." Mrs. Jacobs rolls her handout into a scroll and points it at us. "Who was the leader in the *Amistad* revolt?"

Troy's hand shoots up and startles me. "Joseph Cinque!"

Mrs. Jacobs nods. "Correct."

Troy's such a history junkie. He's always turning his papers in early and doing extra credit. But my Hunky Chunky can't help it if he's got a thing for yesterday's news.

Mrs. Jacobs fires off another question. "What was the role of the sixth president of the United States, John Quincy Adams, in the *Amistad* case?"

I ease my butt to the left again, lean, slump, and rotate, just so I can check on Troy. He's looking at baseball cards, just like he does every day at this time. Since he made the baseball team, I'm thinking about going to a game or two. I bet he looks All-Star awesome in his uniform. And knowing he loves baseball just makes me crush on him even more.

I can imagine us dressed in matching baseball uniforms, because our skills are just that good, getting ready to take the field for our hometown team. But then, Troy gets on one knee and in front of the umpires and everyone begs me to be his girl. I'll hold my glove close to my heart as he says those magic words:

"Laura Dyson, it would be my honor to carry you inside my dimple and be your Hunky Chunky from now until forever."

"Laura?"

I'd climb inside his dimple and wave like a princess as we take the field to play a game.

"Earth to Laura Dyson!"

And just before I step out of his face, he'll check the pitcher's mound to make sure there aren't any spiders or bugs crawling around to bother me as I pitch.

"LAURA!"

"Huh?"

I tumble out of Troy's dimple and crash back into my history class desk. Mrs. Jacobs looks over the top of her glasses at me.

"Answer the question, please."

I'm a bit lost. "Sure, Mrs. Jacobs, could you repeat it?"

"It's the same question I've been asking for the last two minutes."

Troy's hand is waving like crazy, but I guess Mrs. Jacobs is tired of calling on him. Then Sunny whispers, "Larda's so fat, she was probably daydreaming about an all-you-can-eat buffet," loud enough for me to hear. My classmates giggle, but I ignore them.

Mrs. Jacobs is waiting for an answer, and I'm not positively, no-doubt sure of the question. My heart's beating double time, so I sigh and let it fly.

"Wasn't he, like, a lawyer? I mean seriously, who wasn't a lawyer back then?"

Mrs. Jacobs chuckles. "Sometimes I wonder that exact same thing. *Gracias*, Laura. Thank you!"

I stare at my desk, wishing the bell would ring. If this day goes any slower, it will be yesterday again. A quick glance at the clock tells me it's . . . *RRRRRRRING!*

Books close, seats empty, and soon the hallway fills with a herd of students all moving in the same direction toward their rides home. I inch my way toward the door, and at the first opening in the crowd I merge into traffic.

Finally! The weekend is here! Tomorrow, I'll spend the day with my parents and Aunt Carmen doing something awesome. And then Dad's taking me to the Astros' season opener on Sunday before he and Mom hit the road. I can't wait.

This weekend's got *magnifico* written all over it.

chapter four

I slap a smile on my face and open the front door. I'm about to yell, "I'm home!" when I notice Dad standing in the living room. He's wearing his college baseball jersey, and that's our private code that he wants to go into the backyard and throw the baseball.

I point to my bedroom. "I'll get my glove and meet you outside."

I rush to my room, put on a pair of black sweats, and grab my glove. In less than five minutes, I'm opening the patio door.

"Where's Mom?"

Dad reaches into a bucket and grabs a bright white

baseball with RAWLINGS written on the top and two sets of tight red laces stitched around the seams. There's a stamp in the center that reads OFFICIAL MAJOR LEAGUE BASEBALL, with the signature of the baseball commissioner right underneath it. Dad says if the ball doesn't have all that stuff on it, it ain't worth throwing.

"Your mom's in the study making calls, sending faxes. You know how she gets."

I frown. "She's *still* faxing? I know she faxed a bunch of stuff to the office at school. I was there when it came in."

Dad's eyes zoom into mine. "Then you already know?"

I shrug. "Know what?"

His smile is weak. "Let's just throw soft pitches right now. We both need to warm up."

My knower's stirring, making me focus on everything about Dad. His walk has dread in it, as if he's got something heavy weighing him down. I grind my fist into the palm of my glove, ready to help him any way I can. Soon he'll toss the ball and tell me what's on his mind. That's how he gets things off his chest. He catches. I pitch. He talks. I listen. Problems get solved.

That's how we roll.

Dad squats in a catcher's position and arcs the ball to me. "We may be here awhile."

I toss it back. We play this game of silent soft toss

until I'm sick of it.

"Okay, Dad, we've warmed up enough. What do you want me to throw?"

He opens his glove. "Throw me a curveball, because that's what I'm about to throw you."

I tilt my head and stare at him. "What does that mean?"

"Just throw the curveball, Laura."

So I do. He catches it and stuns me. "Carmen's not coming. Throw another curveball."

He arcs the ball to me again. I squeeze it in my hand and try to digest what Dad's saying. With two fingers around the laces, I wind up and throw what he wants, then shrug.

"Okay. Do we have to go pick her up?"

Dad rubs his thumb across the ball. "No. Carmen's not coming at all because she's getting married tomorrow. Throw a changeup."

My brain locks. "What are you talking about?"

Dad shakes his head. "We've had to make other plans. Let me see that changeup."

I glare at the ball. Throw a changeup? Aunt Carmen bailing on me is the worst changeup ever. And the more I think about it, the tighter I squeeze the ball.

"Isn't this like . . . her twentieth marriage or something? Okay, I know that's not true, but why can't she get married *next* month? I thought you talked to her about this weeks ago?"

Dad nods. "I did. But this new guy in her life proposed yesterday. He's taking her to the Little Wedding Chapel in Las Vegas and they're getting married tonight. Carmen said he's paying for everything, including the honeymoon suite at the Bellagio. She sends her apologies to you, but she said she knew you'd understand."

I *don't* understand. I swipe my hand over my face, hoping to rub away the anger, but it won't go.

"Throw the changeup, Laura."

I shake my head. "I don't want to."

Mom slides open the patio door, and our eyes meet. "Hi, Laura. I guess you heard the news." She steps outside and slides the door closed. "Let's sit at the patio table."

I can feel Dad watching us as he walks to the table. Mom gives me a big hug, then retells what I already know about Aunt Carmen. I listen, but I save the most important question for last.

"Then who's coming to stay with me?"

Mom and Dad exchange a look before Mom puts her hand on top of mine. I'm waiting for an answer, but they take too long. So I give a possibility of my own.

"I could stay with the Baxters. I'm always over at Sage's house, spending the night or hanging out.

Mr. and Mrs. Baxter treat me like I'm their other daughter."

Mom rubs my hand. "That's a really good option, Laura, but they're not on the list of caregivers that we gave to the military."

I shrug. "Who is?"

Mom lifts her hand off mine and holds up one finger. "Well, there's Carmen."

I'm waiting for finger number two to rise, but instead, Mom puts her hand back on mine as the edges of her eyes droop.

"The other is your grandma."

There's a numbness working its way up from my toes. "What does that mean?"

Now Dad's looking at Mom as she clears her throat.

"I called my commanding officer and tried to add other relatives, but it's too late. I tried, Laura, but you'll be living with your grandma out on the farm until we get back."

The numbness speeds up my legs and shuts down my whole body. I can't move. My jaws lock. My eyes won't blink. There's got to be a mistake somewhere, and as soon as I un-numb, maybe I can help figure it out. But until then, I manage one word.

"No."

Mom keeps talking. "Look, I know how you feel about the farm."

I pull my hand away from hers. "I can't . . . you don't understand."

Mom keeps talking. "I *do* understand, Laura. I know how much you hate going out there, but we don't have a choice. We had to make a last-minute substitution with absolutely no time to change the caregiver sheet we gave to our superiors."

I'm curling my fingers inside my glove. "I hate it out there, Mom. Come on—there has to be someone else who could stay with me."

"Your grandma loves you, Laura. She's absolutely overjoyed about spending some one-on-one time with you. It'll give you two an opportunity to grow closer."

I keep pleading my case. "All she wants to do is talk about that ridiculous shack and the Laura Line. We don't have one thing in common! And Mom, I'll be miserable. Please, make some more calls. There *has* to be somebody else."

A tear falls from Mom's eye. Dad lowers his head as Mom shuts the door on my hope for a better solution. "There's nothing I can do. I know this is a major surprise for you. Us, too."

I frown. "A surprise? It's the worst news ever! I'm trying to think of what I did that made you so angry that you'd sentence me to Grandma's farm for two whole weeks!"

Mom stands. "You think we're trying to punish you?"

I rub the side of my head. "It'll be the same as being in Mrs. Jacobs's history class after school and all through the night and every weekend! She's talking about slave ships and slaves. Then I'll come home and listen to Grandma talk about that slave shack and all the slaves buried behind it."

Dad touches my back. "Laura . . ."

I turn to him. "I can't even believe she still *has* that slave shack. Am I the only person who understands how shameful that is? I mean, *ding!* It's embarrassing!"

Now it's my turn to hold up fingers one at a time to make my point. "I'm talking slavery, shackles, beatings, jack-nasty floors, no bathrooms, no air conditioning, and no telling what else! I could never invite friends over, just because of the shack."

Mom turns her palms up so I can see them. "Look, Laura, there is so much more to the shack than slavery. And there's more to the farm than just the shack. Why don't you give it a chance?"

I've got a bad case of angry, and if I don't empty my mind, I just might launch into space. So I lose the glove and let it all out.

"My schoolmates already make fun of me. My nickname is Fat Larda! And I hate school. I bet that was the same feeling our ancestors had about that shack. Just like me, one rotten day after another. Now I have to spend my days taking abuse from my classmates and then go to the farm and spend my nights staring at the original school of cruel."

Mom tugs at her blouse the same way I do, just to make sure it hasn't risen on her. But then she lifts her chin in the air and smiles as if she's proud.

"Is that who you are? Fat Larda?"

Just hearing it fall out of Mom's mouth stings. I give her a quick answer. "No."

She places her hands on my chin and turns my face toward hers.

"Then who are you?"

What kind of question is that for a parent to ask their child? Even though we're still eye-to-eye, there must be a totally different answer she's looking for, and I have no idea what that is. So I don't answer at all. Maybe she's going to answer it for me.

Mom's face softens. "When I come back in two weeks, I want an answer. I don't believe in coincidences, Laura. There's a reason why this change of plans happened at the last minute."

My voice gets louder than I intended. "I wanted Aunt Carmen, not Grandma!"

Dad drops his glove on the table and stands. "Okay, let's take a breath and get back on track. Laura, I've listened to you and now it's time for you to hear me. Your mom and I realize staying with Grandma is not your first choice, but right now, it's your *only* choice. We know you're not happy, but it is what it is and we need to move on. So tomorrow morning start packing, because on Sunday we're heading to Killeen for two weeks and you're going to the farm. This family meeting is over."

The backyard is so quiet that I want to cover my ears. Mom takes her time crossing the yard, then slides the patio door open and steps inside. Dad taps me with his mitt.

"Come on, let's finish throwing."

I shake my head. "Not now, Dad."

He hands me my glove and points to the grass. "Yes, now!"

The bass in his voice startles me. I scoot back and tromp across the grass to my side of the yard, clenching the ball in one hand with my glove on the other.

Dad stoops at the other end of the yard with his mitt open and ready. I wait for his pitch signal. He shows me two fingers. Normally that would be a curveball, but right now, he's going to get something with a little sting to it. I wind up and throw as hard as I can with a loud grunt.

Umph . . . POP!!!

He takes his mitt off, checks his hand, and glares at me. "I called for a curveball. You must've missed the signal."

I don't answer. Instead, I hold my glove out for him to throw the ball back. He arcs one to me and then signals for another curveball.

Umph . . . POP!!!

He glares at me again and tosses the ball back without saying a word. For the next six pitches, I pound the inside of his mitt with heat, one fiery fastball after another. But just before the seventh pitch, my arm falls to my side as the ball rolls out of my glove and into the grass. My head bobs short nods as I try to stay in control of my emotions. But I can't.

Dad rushes to me and holds my face to his chest as tears soak his jersey.

"There it is, Laura. That's what I was looking for. Let it all out. And who knows, maybe this whole thing will be better than we ever imagined."

I move away from him, open the patio door, and rush to my room. In less than an hour, this weekend's outlook changed from blue skies with a 100-percent chance of awesome to hurricane warnings. I was counting on hanging out with my *magnifica* Aunt Carmen.

Instead, I get my *loca* grandma for two long weeks.

But the worst has to be that now, on top of keeping my regular secrets like the snacks in my backpack, baseball, and my love for Troy Bailey, I've got a big-time shack-shaking, joke-making secret to keep. I can't believe this! I'm leaving a first-class house to live on a second-rate farm.

This shack has to stay under the radar. If I slip up, it could be my biggest mistake ever. I won't let that happen. Heck to the tenth power of no way.

chapter five

Ever since dad showed me how to pitch, I've been hooked on the game. One day he ordered pizza and we watched the Astros play the Dodgers on TV together. I didn't know any of the players from either team, so it was kind of hard to follow along. But those teams played three games against each other that weekend, and soon I began to recognize the players' names.

The only people who know how I feel about baseball are Sage and my parents. It's kind of like a superhero story: At school, I'm disguised as an exceptionally smart . . . uh . . . cool student. But at home, Laura Dyson stands in the backyard with her glove on one hand and throws fire and ice, depending on her mood.

Who cares? I reach into my drawer and grab my secret stash of mini Almond Joys. Dang. I've only got five left. They've got to last me. I throw the bag into my luggage, close the top, and sit on my bed.

Knock-knock.

"Come in."

Dad peeks in and smiles. "You don't have any baseballs in here to throw at me, do you? I mean, my hand is still stinging from yesterday. Besides, I brought you a peace offering."

Dad hands me a tuna sandwich. I give him a half grin, take a bite, then shrug. "Thanks for the sandwich, but what about tomorrow's Astros game?"

Dad closes the door and sits next to me. "Now that we're taking you to your grandma's house, that's extra travel time to Killeen that we hadn't counted on. Plus, your mother's already upset about this whole change of plans. She'll want to talk with you and with Grandma before we leave. That's probably another hour or two lost. So—"

I interrupt him. "I'm not going, right?"

He puts his arm around me. "I didn't say that."

I perk up. "Then who's taking me?"

"I think the game would be a great way for you and your grandma to get to know each other a little better. I mean, even though we eat Sunday dinner with her every week on the farm, you don't spend much time alone with her."

I drop the sandwich back on the plate. "Because I don't like sitting around listening to stories about that shack, especially when Grandma always stops in the middle of the stories and spaces out. It seems as if it doesn't matter where the conversation starts, it always ends up about the shack or the Laura Line. And I don't have a big-time crush on that stuff like she does."

Dad nods. "I understand. But actually, your grandma's looking forward to taking you to the game. Eat your sandwich."

I take another bite. There's a tell-all silence in my room, a stillness that says everything without a single word. The longer I stare at Dad, the more he shrugs. Finally he just kills the silence.

"It was her or nothing, Laura. I know she doesn't understand the game."

I interrupt. "She'll fall asleep and snore ten minutes after 'The Star-Spangled Banner.'"

Dad tightens his lips and closes his eyes before answering. "Maybe not."

But I keep going. "I'll have to take her to the bathroom after every inning. And she'll want coffee instead of a Coke like what we drink."

Dad puts his arm around me. "There's nothing

wrong with coffee. Let her have it."

"She'll complain about the prices and probably try to give her coffee back, right in front of everybody. I'll be so embarrassed, Dad. Maybe we just shouldn't go."

He hugs me closer. "Listen, Laura, you're the only person I know who understands the pitchers' duel that's going down tomorrow. Don't let your grandma stop you from seeing that! Plus I want a play-by-play report from you. Now eat that sandwich, then finish packing. I love you."

I put my head on his shoulder. "Love you, too." Reality comes in the form of pain as I think about how much I'm going to miss him and Mom. And I don't even have enough time to deal with it.

Early Sunday morning, Dad takes the last of my luggage to the car, but I don't follow him. I'm staring at myself in the mirror, dressed in my classic orange, yellow, and red striped Astros jersey, jeans, and orange Sketchers to pull the outfit together.

But I'm not excited, and it shows in the mirror. How pathetic am I that I would agree to go with my grandma—who knows nothing about baseball—just to see a game.

Mom calls out to me. "Let's go, Laura. Your dad and I have a long ride ahead. It's going to take us thirty minutes just to get to your grandma's house."

"Coming." I grab my glove, leave my bedroom, and close the door. This is so wrong.

I'm surprised when Mom opens the door behind Dad and sits next to me in the backseat. She gives me a smile and I force one back. As Dad drives down Main Street, my eyes fix on Wildflower Mall. I put my hand to the window, wondering how long it will be before I shop with Sage again. Will new stores open while I'm gone? Will my favorite stores close?

Then we pass the movie theater. A whole new loss rumbles in my stomach. Does Grandma even have cable? Now that I'm thinking about it, I wonder what Grandma cooks during the week. I've been to her house for family dinners when she had pot roast or barbecued ribs, but what does she cook on Mondays? Or Tuesdays?

I unzip my backpack and grab a pack of gum. Mom's looking at me, so I offer her a piece, and she takes it. Even though it's just a simple piece of sugar-free spearmint, it's the one thing we can agree on right now.

Soon the city fades to open spaces of nothing and the speed limit lowers to forty.

I think that speed change is a slick way to warn people of what's ahead. But to me, there are three monster clues for city folk to realize they've just entered a time-travel rewind:

1. The street name changes from Main to Ennis Trail;
2. The speed limit drops again, from forty to twenty; and
3. Instead of two lanes, we merge into one wide strip of asphalt with no yellow line down the middle to divide the traffic.

The beautiful buildings disappear. Now wooden fences line the road. Stop signs replace traffic lights. Since we're only going twenty miles an hour, it feels as if we're driving in the longest school zone ever. While Dad rolls to a stop, I look out of my window in time to watch a cow stick its tongue inside its nose and glare at us like we're the gross ones.

Soon, Dad makes a turn off of Ennis Trail to Chapel Lane. The smooth asphalt turns to loose gravel. And that's when it hits me: Down this gravel road is where I'll spend two weeks of my life that I'll never get back. And the more Dad's tires crunch that gravel, the more it feels like it's me under those tires, getting crushed and broken into little pieces of nothing.

Mom presses a button and her window slides down. "Mmm, I love the smell of country air. It brings back so many memories."

Dad inhales. "Doesn't it smell wonderful, Laura?"

I cover my nose and Dad pulls over into the grass on the side of the gravel road and turns off the ignition. Both he and Mom turn to me. I slide my hand off my nose.

"What? I didn't say anything! What'd I do?"

Mom speaks up. "Laura, honey, you've made it crystal clear that you don't want to be here. We get it. But your dad and I need you to be strong. We need to concentrate on our military exercises. Do you understand that?"

I lower my head and nod. Mom continues. "We can't be worried about whether you and your grandma are getting along. You've got to promise me you'll try your best."

"I promise."

Now I feel worse. Here they're going to learn more about how to protect the United States and I'm trippin'. So I fake a smile until their expressions change from sad to glad.

"Okay, I can do this. I mean, it's only two weeks, right?"

Dad starts the ignition, then holds out his fist for me to bump. "That's my girl."

Mom leans over and kisses my forehead. "Everything's going to be okay."

When Dad gets back on the gravel road, I gaze out the car window. The more I look, the more I realize this place isn't really a farm. I've read enough books like *Charlotte's Web* and *Click-Clack-Moo* to know that animals make a farm. But I don't see any. And it's too quiet.

Rusty barbed-wire fencing sags from the wooden posts like double Dutch jump rope. With no cattle, no crops, and no tractor, there's really nothing left to even justify this place as anything but a bunch of wasted space.

But I have to say the grass looks great. It always does. For a fake farm, the manicured acres help a bunch. And there's the shack. I turn and look away, but my brain's already taken a snapshot. Even though I'm not looking at it, I can still see it in my mind.

We've reached the top of the hill, and Grandma's old brown Buick rests under a big oak tree. There's a shiny black Jeep Cherokee parked next to her car.

What the what? Grandma's got company? Is she kickin' it with somebody? Mom's going to flip out if she is. Dad eyeballs the SUV as we roll by.

"Honey, you recognize that Jeep?"

Mom shakes her head. "No, I don't know who it belongs to. But I'm going to find out."

Sweet Sister of Secret Hookups! Grandma's got a boyfriend! When Dad stops, I can't get out of the car fast enough. I open the screen and turn the knob on Grandma's door. It opens, and I enter the room, hoping to bust Grandma doing something she shouldn't be doing. I'm grinning to throw off my true intentions.

"Hey, Gr . . ."

Sitting at Grandma's table, dressed in a white blouse, jeans, and boots, is the absolute last person I'd expect to see out here. The rumbling in my stomach turns sour and I accidentally swallow my gum. Grandma shuffles over to me.

"Baby Girl, I'm so excited about you staying here with me. And I'm sure you know my friend Edna. But you call her . . ."

Dad stumbles in with four of my bags. "Sorry we're late. . . ."

Once he makes eye contact with the woman at the table, his head tilts, and that's exactly how I feel when he asks the question that I already know the answer to.

"Aren't you Mrs. Jacobs, my daughter's history teacher?"

chapter six

Mrs. Jacobs's smile is blinding.

"Hey there, Laura!"

I'm numb dumb, staring at my history teacher like she's an alien. Has she seen the shack? Does she know it's out there?

"Uh, hi, Mrs. Jacobs."

She reaches for Grandma's hand and answers the question that's in my head.

"Bet you're wondering what I'm doing here! Me and Laura Lee—I mean your grandmother—have been friends since second grade. We're just so busy that we don't get to see each other as much as we'd like. But we do lots of things together. Today we decided to have brunch so we could finish some business we're working on."

Grandma adds, "That's right. Edna and I have been friends a long time. We were even pregnant at the same time."

I feel that wad of gum practically bouncing back up my throat.

Boing, boing, boing.

Mrs. Jacobs butts in again. "That's right, that's right. Plus your grandma was the maid of honor at my wedding and I was the same at hers."

Grandma grins. "Sure was."

I can't take much more. "Oh, that's really . . . Grandma, where can I put my things?"

She points down the hall. "I thought it'd be fun for you to stay in your mother's old bedroom."

I give her a thumbs-up. "Awesome."

The walls leading down the hall are painted a green I've never seen in any crayon box. It's not gross green or even puke green, but it definitely belongs in the sick-green family. I step inside the bedroom and find that same color of paint on the walls.

I drop my backpack on a small desk not far from an old-timey mirrored dresser. The bed against the wall is much smaller than my queen-size one at home. But there's a window with pretty lace curtains that cast a shadow from the sunlight, and I'm hoping my view will be a billboard on a far-off freeway or maybe even the tall sign of McDonald's. I pull back the curtains and immediately wish I hadn't.

There it is, representing a gazillion different levels of wrong and, worse, the number-one reason I didn't want to come here. It's not fair that the shack is what I see from my window, when all I hoped was to see something that reminded me of home.

Dad comes in with my luggage, and I want to take it back to the car.

"Laura Eboni?"

I stick my head out of the room. It's Mom, signaling for me to come back in the kitchen. I try to eyeball everything in Grandma's kitchen except Mrs. Jacobs as Mom talks.

"We need to leave, but I want you to take a walk with me before I go."

I shrug and fight the urge to cry. "Sure, Mom."

Dad's coming down the hall and I think he's going to stop, but he doesn't. Instead, he touches my shoulder, walks out the door, and closes it.

Mrs. Jacobs stands, takes her purse off of the table, and hugs Grandma. "Well, Laura Lee, I know you've got a big-time baseball game to go to, so I'm going to leave. I've got to go over my lesson plan for the week. Bye, everybody! And Laura, I'll see you in class tomorrow."

"Okay."

Mom holds the door open for Mrs. Jacobs, then turns to me.

"Let's go."

We walk toward the woods, not far from the house. Mom puts her arm around my shoulder. Suddenly she stops and stands in front of me. Oh, no. If she starts crying then I will, too. I cross my arms over my stomach. Mom blinks a thousand times before smoothing my hair.

"Don't forget to put conditioner in your hair once a week."

I nod. "I'll remember."

Her hand slides from my hair down the side of my face to my eyebrows.

"Keep your room tidy, and help your grandma when she asks you."

"I will."

"And don't forget the baby powder after you shower and dry off. That helps . . ."

". . . to keep me from misting. I know, Mom."

And then she surprises me. "The ride to school is about twenty-five minutes. But the walk to the mailbox should only take you fifteen, max. It's actually a nice little workout."

My head snaps to the left where she's standing. "Walk to the mailbox? Workout? What are you talking about?"

She shrugs like it's no big deal. "That's where the school bus will pick you up—at the mailbox. Now, you're all set."

I plant my hands on my hips. "You never said anything about me walking to a school bus!" I look down the hill. There's millions of rocks on that gravel road. That's going to ruin my Sketchers. And how far is it from here to the mailbox? Five miles?

Mom smiles. "From your grandma's house to the mailbox is less than a mile, Laura. And it's a beautiful walk, especially this time of the year. Snakes are still hibernating and . . ."

My hands clinch my chest. "Snakes! What the what? Oh heck to the double no! The deal is off! I can't do this."

Mom pulls one of my hands close to her. "Yes, you can! Now listen, you promised. And walking is great exercise. By Wednesday, you'll be looking forward to that walk."

"But I'll be dead by Tuesday!"

"Calm down, Laura. I know it's a lot different from what you're used to, but I bet by the time your dad and I get back, you'll be in love with this place." Mom looks around and breathes in big air. "I know I am. I miss living out here."

I breathe deep too, just to get over the belly bombs exploding inside. But then I notice we're moving closer to the shack. I'm misting more than ever. Sweat is running down my back and making my blouse stick to my skin. I nudge Mom.

"You're not trying to ease me in there, are you?"

Mom looks straight ahead. "No, no, not at all. It's just that the shack brings back memories for me. You know, I did my first science experiment in there. Test tubes and everything."

I look the other way, except now I'm watching Mrs. Jacobs back her Jeep up. I can't take it. I wipe the mist beading on my face.

"Mom, I'm freaking out. I mean, I walk into Grandma's house and my history teacher is all cozy at the kitchen table. And she's swinging a shiny black Jeep Cherokee like somebody in a rap video. Then you give me this 'Oh, by the way, you've got a new workout plan. It's called walk until you die,' and I'm supposed to be okay with it?"

Dad's voice startles me. "Okay with what?"

I turn to him. "Did you know I have to walk twenty miles to the bus stop?"

His eyebrows move close together. "Stop exaggerating, Laura. It's a short walk. And if we were still at home, you'd be walking from the house to the bus. Here it's just a little farther. Anyway, come with me. I've got something to show you."

Mom and I follow Dad into a wooded area away

from the house and the shack. The trees are tall, with lots of room between them. I'm watching everywhere, just to be sure there are no sleepless snakes around. But soon, I get a glimpse at where we're going and my walking slows on its own.

In the middle of the woods is a tree that stands away from the others. Nailed to it is a huge board with a white square in the center. Just barely above the white square is Dad's glove, opened and ready for a pitch. He walks toward the target, and I follow him as he talks.

"This felt like a good spot for home plate."

My walk's mechanical as I take in what Dad has done. I try to listen while I look.

"I've given this a lot of thought, Laura. So instead of nailing my glove to the tree for you to use as a target, I decided to rig it so it can slide left and right above home plate. This way you can practice all of your pitches, not just the ones that come straight down the middle. You like it? I even made you a mound. It's just a couple bags of dirt with an old piece of tarp over it, so be careful."

A pitcher's mound! I rush to it and examine my view from there. Behind me are lots of trees. They're tall, just like I'd want my teammates to look like on defense. I turn back to the lone tree where Dad nailed home plate. Behind that one tree is a long fence of chopped wood.

On the other side of the chopped wood are more trees, all different sizes. Some of the tree trunks are big, some skinny. Others are short with lots of branches and leaves, while a few are bare. The trees look like they're watching me. Not in a creepy way, but the same way people watch a baseball game. I want to tell Dad exactly what this means to me, but I don't think the words I'm looking for are in a dictionary.

It's like Christmas in December collided with my birthday in August and gave me this megavalentine from February . . . in April.

Sweet Brother of Baseball. Dad built me my very own stadium.

"This is crazy! I can't believe you made this just for me. I absolutely love it."

He grabs a bucket from behind the tree and sets it down at my feet. Inside the bucket are baseballs and my glove. Before he can say a word, I wrap my arms around him, close my eyes, and think about how lucky I am to have parents who understand me. Then he whispers.

"Laura Eboni, whenever things get too hard or you have trouble figuring something out, come here and throw until it makes sense, okay?"

I grab my glove from the bucket and smile.

Tears make their way down Mom's face. She pulls me to her and holds tight.

"I'm going to miss you."

"I'm going to miss you, too, Mom. Don't worry about me and Grandma. You concentrate on what you're doing, okay?"

Dad kisses my cheek as Mom holds me. "I love you. Everything's going to be fine."

Then he reaches for Mom's arm. "Come on, honey, we've got to get on the road."

Watching my parents leave is much harder than I'd imagined. Even with Grandma standing next to me, I feel alone and scared. Once they turn onto the gravel road and their car disappears, the farm seems to double in size. Grandma takes my hand.

"And we've got a ball game to catch. Meet me at the car. I'll get my keys."

"Grandma, how much do you know about baseball?"

She wrinkles her face as if she tasted something she didn't like.

"Not much, but as long as I can get a cup of coffee in between the action, I'll be fine. Maybe you can teach me. Yeah! I want to learn everything about baseball."

A spark of energy hits me. "I can totally teach you!"

She turns back to me. "Perfect! I've made some pork chop sandwiches for us, in case we get hungry."

I frown. "You can't bring food or drinks from home into the ballpark, Grandma. Security will check your purse."

Her eyes widen. "That's nonsense! I'll figure out something."

As I beat my fist inside my glove, the excitement builds, knowing I'm on my way to Minute Maid Park to see my Astros play. And even though Dad's not going, Grandma *did* say she wanted to learn about the game. I rub the inside of my glove, then pound it some more.

This is a good game for me to teach her. I can't help but grin thinking about today's pitching matchup. And I get to watch it live and in person!

I wish Dad was coming, because I know this game is going to be unforgettable.

chapter seven

When we arrive at Minute Maid Park, the place is crawling with baseball fans. Soon, we're at the front of the line and give our tickets to the man at the gate.

"Please step over to the table so Security can check your purse."

Grandma clutches her purse to her stomach. "Check my purse for what?"

He shrugs. "We don't allow any weapons, video equipment, or outside food or drinks inside the stadium. It's standard procedure, ma'am."

Grandma sighs. "That sure seems like an invasion

of my privacy."

I close my eyes, cross my fingers, and don't say a word as the security guard puts both hands inside Grandma's purse and moves stuff to the left and then to the right.

He smiles, then points inside the stadium. "Enjoy the game."

I exhale. "Come on—we have to find our seats. I don't want to miss the first pitch."

We've got great seats in the mezzanine section, which is close enough to maybe snag a foul ball. As the stadium starts to fill up, I can't sit still. There's a man selling pink and blue cotton candy. One lady carries flags with ASTROS written on the front. Another man with a box strapped to his shoulders shouts, "Cold drinks! Get your cold drinks here!"

I turn to Grandma. "This is going to be so fun."

We stand for "The Star-Spangled Banner" and watch fireworks light up the sky when they get to the part about the *rockets' red glare* and *bombs bursting in air*. Once the song's over, the announcer introduces the starting lineups. I clap for every Astro he mentions, and Grandma claps, too. Then I point at the field.

"How about I explain things as they happen? It'll be easier that way."

She nods. "Good idea."

The first inning gets underway, and I explain everything, even the pitches. "Did you see how that pitch started off kind of high and then it just died, like the bottom fell out of it? That's called a sinker."

"Okay, a sinker. That makes sense."

When the Astros come to bat, I do the same thing, except when a low curveball gets called a strike, I lose it and let the umpire know.

"Come on, Blue! That pitch was outside the strike zone! It was a ball!"

Grandma tugs on my jersey. "Why'd you call him Blue?"

I keep watching the game. "His uniform color."

"Oh. I'll just sit and watch for a while. Maybe I'll pick up a few things on my own."

Grandma falls asleep during the second inning and snores until the seventh. I've had a blast watching one of the best pitching matchups ever. But it's time for Grandma to wake up.

I nudge her. "Grandma, it's time for the seventh inning stretch, and somebody's going to sing 'God Bless America.' Look down on the field, Grandma. There's a real person getting ready to lead the singing, not some piped-in organ music blaring through the speakers."

As everybody sings "God Bless America," I think about my parents and hope they're safe. But after the song is over, everything goes south.

Grandma's sneezing, sniffling, and blowing her nose so loudly that it sounds like a bullhorn. "Grandma, are you okay?"

She grabs a small container of hand sanitizer from her purse.

"Allergies. Something in here is setting them off." She leans toward me and whispers, "Hungry?"

I see the hot dog man coming our way. "I'm starving! Can I have . . ."

It seems to happen in slow motion as I watch Grandma reach inside her top and pull out two pork chop sandwiches in Ziplock bags. She hands one to me.

"I'm so glad I didn't put these in my purse. Mmmm, and they're still warm, too."

I'm scared to take that bag, but the sandwich looks so good. As I reach for it, she says something that has me even more worried.

"Thirsty?"

Oh, heck to the triple no! Where is she hiding drinks? Wherever they are, I bet they're not cold.

"No, I'm not thirsty."

Grandma breaks off a piece of her sandwich. "Baby Girl, you're going to love my pork chops. I let them bake in the oven all morning."

I free my sandwich from that bag, and just as I

open my mouth to take a bite, a very tall, thin man in a red jacket, with a walkie-talkie hooked to his pants, makes his way over to us.

"Excuse me, ladies, personal food is not allowed in the ballpark. Please dispose of it."

Grandma's eyes widened. "You mean throw it away? Young man, do you know how much a pound of pork chops costs these days?"

The attendant frowns. "Look, ma'am, those are the rules. Either throw the sandwiches away or you'll have to leave the park."

I frown to match his. "You don't have to be so mean to her! I'm sure she's going to . . ."

Before I could finish my sentence, Grandma says the unthinkable.

"Fine. We'll just leave. Let's go, Baby Girl."

"But Grandma . . ."

I point at the field, then back at the scoreless scoreboard, but she's still going off.

"I'm not throwing away two perfectly good sandwiches. And besides, I think that dirt on the field is irritating my allergies. Why do people like this game? It's just a bunch of grown men running around like kids and getting dirty."

I follow her, trying not to step on people's feet as we walk sideways to get out into the aisle.

"But Grandma, the game's not over."

"For us it is."

I've never left a game before it ended, even when my team was getting slaughtered. Reluctantly, I climb in the car, close my door, and try to make sense of what just happened. It takes a moment before I realize Grandma hasn't started the car. I turn to face her. She's staring at me.

"Laura Eboni, what's wrong? You wanted to stay?"

I glance back at Minute Maid Park, and even through my rolled up window, I can hear the cheers. I turn back to Grandma.

"That wasn't an invasion of your privacy at the security check, Grandma. That was for our safety. Then something in the park upset your allergies. Do you have allergy medicine that you're supposed to take? And then you refused to throw away the pork chop sandwiches when *we* were wrong for bringing them in. But to me, the worst is making fun of the ballplayers and how they play the game, because I love baseball."

We're quiet in the car again. Grandma sneezes a few times, but all I'm thinking is that I've missed the eighth inning and am going to miss the ninth, too. She reaches over and rubs my shoulder. She's got that spaced-out look on her face that I've seen so many times when she's talking about the shack or the Laura Line. I'm thinking she's going to say something crazy, but instead, she apologizes.

"I was wrong and I'm sorry. I didn't realize how much you loved baseball. I guess I don't know doodly-squat about you."

I frown, wondering what a doodly-squat is, but the more she talks, the more I get it.

"But that's going to change. And next time, I'll take my allergy medicine, because there will be other games, Baby Girl. I promise."

I think about Dad, because this wasn't just any game. This was his gift to me. If he had come, we would have been the last two people to leave the ballpark. As angry as I want to be, I think of Mom and how I promised her that I'd do my best. So I exhale, take a bite of my sandwich, and lie.

"It's no big deal, Grandma. Really."

After we get home, I stay dressed in my Astros jersey since I'm sure the game's still going on. If I took it off, it'd be as if I *chose* to leave early.

Later, after Grandma's gone to bed, I stand in my new bedroom, looking out the window at the slave shack. It's the first time I've ever seen it at night, and it's got a whole new layer of creepy on it.

Goose bumps cover me, and I close the curtain until there's only a slice of an opening left for me to peek through. I look behind me and all around the room. I think I'll turn on my lamp.

Wait. Maybe I shouldn't, because . . .

What if the shack has night creatures in it, or worse, the soul of every dead slave who's ever lived in there awakens when the sun goes down and the moon comes up? What if at night, slave zombies open up the front door and come searching for food? I change my mind about turning that lamp on. I don't want them to see me and think . . . Mmm, Kentucky fried Laura.

Heck to the double no.

And those six crosses behind it, lit up by the moon, make that whole area crazy scary right now. Even though I know the crosses represent each Laura in my ancestry who's dead, it's still spooky to me. The Laura Line. What a silly name for a graveyard.

BZZZZZ. BZZZZZZZZZZZ.

Aack! It's the slave zombies! I run around the room, slapping at my jeans pocket, trying to get whatever's buzzing my leg off me! Oh. Wait. I reach into my pocket, pull out my phone, and read the highlighted words ANSWER or IGNORE. It's Dad.

"Laura? Did the Astros win? I was listening on the radio but lost the signal."

My heart's still racing, but I manage to catch my breath. Then I roll my eyes thinking about what happened at the ballpark. "We left early."

"What?"

"Grandma hid pork chop sandwiches in her blouse, and we got kicked out."

I can tell he's covered the phone with his hand. I think he's laughing but I'm not sure. Finally, he moves his hand and talks to me.

"Well, I'm sorry to hear that. Hang in there. Training exercises begin for your mom and me at oh-six-hundred hours, so I've got to go. Don't forget to throw. I love you."

"Love you, too, Dad. Tell Mom I love her, too. Bye."

I flop across the bed. This has been the worst weekend ever. And my forecast for tomorrow is a 100-percent chance of the same as today. I've got nothing in common with my grandma. And on top of that, I'll have to hike across the world to the bus stop, all the while avoiding anacondas and probably bears, too.

But no matter what happens, I've got to try to keep my promise. And I can do it, because I learned a lot about myself tonight. If I can leave a baseball game early over a pork chop sandwich without causing a scene, there's absolutely nothing that can shake me.

chapter eight

"Mornin', Laura."

Grandma's voice reminds me where I am as I walk into the kitchen.

"Good morning, Grandma. Bacon smells good."

"Pull up a chair. I've got scrambled eggs, bacon, homemade biscuits with apple butter, and fresh-squeezed orange juice."

Sweet Brother of Breakfast Buffets! "I don't eat like this at home. Mom leaves so early."

Grandma sips her coffee. "If she had time, your mom would cook like this, too."

I stab a forkful of eggs. "So you're saying Mom

knows how to throw down like this?"

"Of course! It's in the Line, Baby Girl. One of the first Lauras, Laura Belle, owned her own restaurant. People crowded her place, especially on Sundays after church. She left us some of her secret recipes. They're in the shack. You should check it out."

Did I just walk into a shack trap? I keep eating without looking up. "Uh-huh . . ."

Grandma keeps on. "Just in case you ever want to take a look at it, the ledger of the Laura Line is in the shack. I don't ever take it out."

I pick up my orange juice. "Uh-huh."

An invisible wall rises as silence lurks between us. I rush to finish my breakfast.

"Thanks, Grandma. That was awesome."

She nods. "You know, Laura, if you're scared about going in the shack, I'd be . . ."

I should have known this breakfast had a catch. But I didn't see it coming. I push back from the table, because now is as good a time as any to take a stand.

"Grandma, I don't want to talk about the shack, okay? I'm . . . I'm just not interested."

There. I said it. I'm expecting a fight, but instead, she nods and smiles. "I understand better than you think I do. And it's okay. But I want you to remember that it's never too late to learn something new. I've just got a feeling today is going to be special for you. Do you want me to make you a lunch?"

"No, I buy my lunch at school."

I keep looking at her. Is it over? Did we argue? I feel like I'm wearing boxing gloves for a marshmallow fight. And she's smiling at me! What the what? And how does she know my day is going to be special? I don't know what to say, so I just back up toward my room. Grandma calls out to me.

"Wear flat shoes for that walk to the bus stop!"

I'm out of the house in no time, wearing my flats like Grandma suggested, but I can feel every pebble underneath my soles. I don't need flats; I need Mom's army boots.

It's only been a few minutes, but I'm breaking a mist tromping through this gravel. I'll be all sticky before I even get to school. Between the trees, I can see the shack. I'd recognize that ugly wood anywhere. But I slow down when I see the six crosses behind it. The sun shines on them like spotlights, as if they were some big-time movie stars.

But they weren't.

If the Laura Line was all that, everybody would know about them. I'd be Laura of the famous Laura Line instead of just Fat Larda of the infamous nobodies.

Mom was right about one thing. It took me fifteen minutes to walk from Grandma's house to this mailbox, and here comes the bus. Brakes squeal to a halt, the doors open, and the driver smiles.

"Mornin'."

"Hi," I say.

I recognize the driver, but I'm too tired from the walk to care. I'm the first person aboard, and I get to pick where I want to sit. I choose in the middle so I can see everybody when they get on. I'm looking all around, as if this bus may have something different from mine. Then my eyes freeze on a spot. Above the driver's head, I see the number.

189. That's Sage's bus. And . . .

Up ahead a boy with a backpack walks toward a mailbox as the bus slows down. I recognize that strut and smash my face against the window to get a better look. Could it . . . Yes!

It's Troy.

I smooth my hand across the top of my head to make sure I don't have any strands sticking straight up in the air. Do I have farm frizz? I check my shoes for gravel dust. I'm sure I look a mess.

The bus stops and so does my heart. And when Troy climbs the steps and stands near the driver, I hear an orchestra play a love song.

Do I have lip gloss on? I'm so worried about how I look that it takes a second for the real fear to creep into my brain.

Does he know about the shack?

The bus driver greets him. "Mornin', Troy."

Troy bumps fists with the driver, then heads down the aisle. He hesitates when we make eye contact, but he doesn't speak. So I do.

"Hi, Troy."

He nods, says, "Hey," and keeps walking.

My left knee bounces as I wipe mist from my forehead. Okay, did he say "hey" or "hi"? Did he mean it or was he just trying to be polite? Sweet Mother of Chocolate Hunky Chunkies, he looked right at me!

I get more looks as students get on. It's as if I'm the new kid . . . or a zoo animal. But when Sage gets on the bus, everything changes. I see her from my window, standing in line behind a bunch of popular students, including Sunny Rasmussen. I'm so busy looking at Sunny that I don't notice Shane Doyles coming down the aisle.

"What are you doing on this bus, Larda?"

I frown at him. "Sitting. Isn't that what you should be doing?"

He strolls toward the back and hollers, "Yo, Troy, we got a hippo on the bus!"

Two weeks of Shane Doyles's mouth may be more than I can handle. But I forget about him when I see Sage make her way up the steps. She turns sideways and shuffles down the aisle because her hips are too wide to walk the regular way without touching people. As she scoots down the aisle, she jiggles a bit, and kids exaggerate moving out of her way. I watch the reaction of guys and girls after she goes by them. They stare, point, and snicker. Did they do that behind *my* back on my regular bus?

When our eyes meet, Sage moves faster down the aisle, talking as she makes her way to me.

"What are you doing on my bus? Where's your aunt Carmen? Did your parents leave? I'm completely blown away seeing you here. Why didn't you tell me?"

I grin. "Surprise! I like this bus, considering where I'm living these days."

Sunny catches my attention near the front of the bus. "Is that Fat Larda?"

"The name's Laura," I say, then move my stuff so Sage can sit.

Sunny rolls her eyes. "You don't live in our neighborhood now, do you?"

She doesn't wait for me to go off on her. Instead, she strolls to the back.

Sage puts her backpack in her lap. "Okay, back up a minute. What do you mean by 'where I'm living these days'?"

I fight an urge to cry. "Aunt Carmen was a no-show. I'm staying with Grandma."

Sage's eyes widen. "No way. Are you all right?"

I shrug. "I think so. Did I mention that I have to walk to the bus stop?"

Sage's eyes widen. "Down that long gravel road? You poor thing!"

I dig deep into my mental database for a comparison Sage would understand.

"It's like I started at Macy's in the mall, hiked all the way down to Penney's, turned around, and walked to the food court, all without stopping."

Sage tries to cheer me up. "Well, maybe it'll help you lose some . . . you know."

When the bus pulls up to our school, Sage and I stand to move into the aisle, but no one lets us out. So we have to wait for everybody, including all the guys from the back, to get off. I sneak another look at Troy when he passes, and I think he looked at me! Once we're off the bus, Sage and I walk inside and down the hall toward our restroom.

Just before we turn the corner, I spot Mrs. Jacobs. She waves, and I give her the limpest wave back. When she steps inside the teachers' break room, I pick up my pace. Sage tries to keep up.

"What now?"

I wait until we're inside our restroom before I break the news.

"There's something else I forgot to tell you.

Yesterday when I got to my Grandma's house, Mrs. Jacobs was there. Turns out her and my Grandma are the world's original BFFs."

Sage closes her eyes. "Shut . . . Up."

I unzip my backpack and search for my lip gloss. "I know, right? What are the odds?"

Sage puts her hand on my shoulder. "Relax. Don't worry. I got your back. You're probably all hyped up for nothing. But I've got a major secret to tell you."

I find my lip gloss, hold it in my hand, and turn to Sage. "Spill it."

Sage begins to pace. "I was standing at the bus stop this morning with Sunny, and she asked me if I'd be interested in joining the Pink Chips."

I flip my wrist at her. "They're nothing but a bunch of fakes."

Sage puts a hand up. "That's not the point. They own this school. And now I've got a shot at being popular! And if I make it, *we* can finally add people to *our* group of friends."

Even though I don't want it to be the Pink Chips, just the idea of other girls hanging out with us sounds great. But then a major question pops into my head, so I ask it.

"I'm not trying to be ugly, Sage, but do you know *why* they asked you?"

Sage talks with her hands. "Well, this morning,

Sunny mentioned the Pink Chips needed a personal photographer. And if I was in their group, they wouldn't have to pay for those really expensive pictures at the mall."

I can't control how wide my eyes open. "What?"

Sage puts her hand on my shoulder. "Wait. She's right! Those pictures *are* expensive! Sunny said after I've been a member for a while and get to know them better, she thought I might do a few articles in the *Crier* about them. I can do that!"

"Sage . . ."

She can't hear me because she's already making plans.

"Laura, I'm going to need your help. You think I should do something different with my hair? I'm definitely going to need a couple of new outfits so I won't look . . . you know."

I shake my head. "You can't be serious! Think about it, Sage. You live in the same neighborhood as Sunny, ride the same bus, go to the same school, and she didn't even know your name. I hope you told her to take a long leap off a short bridge."

Sage frowns at me. "What's wrong with you? Why can't you be happy for me? For the first time ever, people won't call me . . . you know. They'll see me as a Pink Chip."

I exhale. "Sage, all I'm trying to say is—"

She gets louder. "Sometimes you can be so selfish! I've always got your back. Now the biggest thing ever happens for me and you shoot it down. Maybe you're just jealous!"

She tromps out of the restroom. I call out to her. "Sage, wait! That's not true!"

I rush a coat of lip gloss across my lips just as the warning bell rings. It's not the first warning that's sounded in my head today. Between Grandma, Mrs. Jacobs, and Sage, I've got enough drama to last forever.

And none of it feels special.

chapter nine

I eat lunch alone. Sage is a few tables away, sitting by herself, too. I can feel her looking my way and I want to apologize even though I haven't changed my mind about the Pink Chips.

I need chocolate.

So I pick up my tray and head for the conveyer belt. I've got time to go eat an Almond Joy somewhere. On my way, I spot Troy sitting with his friends. It's a table full of Blue Chips, which is the guy version of Pink Chips. Just as I put my tray on the conveyer belt, I hear him say, ". . . Fat Larda on our bus and Shane yelled . . ."

Our eyes meet as his friends pound the table laughing. I rush out of the cafeteria and hurry down the hall to the restroom Sage and I use, fighting tears and wondering what the heck is wrong with me. I like Troy so much it hurts.

He's the reason I come to school every day. Even though I know I'm going to get teased and talked about, I show up just to see him. I think I might like Troy more than I like myself.

I'm in the restroom only seconds before Sage comes in.

"Laura! You okay? Why'd you rush out of the cafeteria?"

"I didn't feel well."

We stand in front of the wall-long mirror and stare at ourselves. Sage holds her brush, but she's not using it. I bet we're thinking the same thoughts. We definitely have the same sad expression. Look at us: two overweight girls, wishing we weren't. And my doctor claims I'm perfect. He says on the growth and weight chart I'm at the high end of normal for girls my age. Sage doesn't talk about her doctor visits. And I don't ask.

The bell rings and I turn to her. "Look, about this morning . . ."

She raises her brush and tames a few hairs on my head.

"Forget about it. You know I can't stay mad at you. We'll talk more later."

She turns to me, and I put my hand on her shoulder. She puts her hand on mine and says, "I will always . . ."

I finish it. " . . . have your back."

We wipe imaginary dust off each other's shoulders and giggle.

Sage leads the way out. "See you after school, Laura."

"Thanks, Sage."

After working in the office during fifth period, I step into Mrs. Jacobs's class and wait for Troy like I always do. When he steps in, he looks my way but quickly turns his head. I try to let him know that I'm not mad at him.

"Hi, Troy. Crazy Monday, right?"

He gives me his regular response. "Hey."

As everyone begins to file in, I notice Troy staring out the window. Sunny is talking to London, another Pink Chip, and everybody else is texting.

When the bell rings, Mrs. Jacobs writes the names of those four children—Kali, Teme, Kagne, and Margru—on the board. To me, that means the *Amistad* is still afloat. I'm so sick of hearing about slaves and fights, especially since I'm living next to the shack now. And that shack makes me think how terrible life had to be for my ancestors.

How many times did they go to bed hungry? How often did the slave owner come inside the shack and beat them with a whip? How many times did they cry themselves to sleep? But the biggest question has to be:

Why would Grandma keep this shame shack and try to play it off as something great?

I wonder if any of them died in there.

My thoughts get the best of me and I raise my hand.

"May I go to the restroom?"

Mrs. Jacobs checks her watch. "Hurry back."

I rush out of the room and down the hall. I waste as much time as I can, getting a drink from the fountain, peeking into other classrooms, and spending a few minutes in the restroom.

I take my sweet time going back. While I'm in the hall, the air conditioner kicks on and the breeze blows my hair. A few strands from my pigtails come loose and the air waves them back and forth across my forehead. I wonder if I resemble one of those models on the magazine covers, looking all awesome with random strands of hair dancing in the wind.

All the Pink Chips have hair that blows with the

slightest breeze. And I've noticed when their hair is blowing, they walk differently and even make diva faces. When I become a big-time fashion model, I'm going to walk differently, too. Hey, what's wrong with practicing?

Maybe if I pooch my lips and tilt my head back a little, I can vogue as I walk by the trophy case glass. Oh, yeah, look at me on the catwalk, modeling an outfit from Paris . . .

Boomph!

I fall off the runway and land back in front of the trophy case, fuming that someone ruined my imaginary modeling debut.

So I blast them before turning around. "Why don't you—"

Troy finishes my sentence. "Watch where you're going!"

I open my eyes.

"Oh, sorry. I . . . I didn't see you."

He rubs his arm. "Obviously."

Troy's talking to me! I scramble for something to say. I've got to keep him talking.

"Where are you going? Bathroom break?"

What the what? I can't believe I just asked him that.

He holds up a yellow slip. "Office visit."

I shift my weight to one leg and smile. "What'd they get you for?"

He walks by me. "Picking up the house key my Dad left for me. Is that a crime?"

I'm feeling lower than a pregnant snake right now, but then Troy really rattles me.

"Mrs. Jacobs is making some big announcement as soon as I come back from the office. She said if I saw you, I should tell you to hurry up."

"Okay, thanks."

Is she retiring? I rush back to class. Mrs. Jacobs looks my way and goes fluent in Eye-ish. I understand completely and apologize with some Eye-ish of my own.

Soon, Troy returns. When Mrs. Jacobs looks away, I pop an Almond Joy into my mouth. There's nothing better than a yummy chocolate snack during a good show. But now I only have four Almond Joys left. If I had known about this earlier, I'd have stashed a bag of popcorn next to my jewelry pouch.

She hands out another stack of papers and has each student in the front row pass them back. It's permission slips for a slavery and freedom research expedition. I hope she didn't find the *Amistad* schooner. Or worse . . . a survivor.

"Okay, class, listen up. I have wonderful news! We've been studying the *Amistad* case for two weeks now, and I thought we'd end this topic of slavery and freedom with a field trip."

My classmates energize, and guesses of where we're going come from every corner of the room. Even though I'd bet one of my Almond Joys that we're going to a museum, I'll still give Mrs. Jacobs props for ending this slave fest by getting us out of school. Maybe it'll be an all-day thing!

There's coconut from my candy stuck to the roof of my mouth because I've sucked all the sweet juices out of those tiny little pieces. They're all dry and I need something to drink, but that's impossible right now because I can't leave class again. Mrs. Jacobs puts a hand in the air.

"Okay, quiet down. I've still got lots of important information to give you."

She's pumped about this field trip, but I wish she'd just tell us and cut the suspense. Finally she lets it fly.

"Since we've been studying slavery, I thought it would be a great idea to see some of the early life of slaves during that time. So not this Friday, but the next one, we're going to the Anderson Farm for a tour of the Double L Slave Shack, guided by none other than our very own Laura Dyson's grandmother, Mrs. Anderson."

I gasp and a cluster of coconut from the roof of my mouth drops on my tonsils and tickles them. A gag forces its way through, and I'm coughing like a cat choking on a hairball.

CACK!

Now, I've got a mouthful of coconut clinging to my tonsils tighter than lint on Velcro.

CACK! CACK!

I try to force the coconut loose with a hard throat clearing. But instead, my throat revs engine sounds similar to jacked-up racecars.

UHUUM-UHUUM!

My watery eyes are full moon wide as Mrs. Jacobs pats my back.

"Are you okay? Were you eating in my class?"

I've got dried, chewed-up coconut pieces scattered across my desk and on the floor. There's some on my blouse. The girl in front of me stares at my cheeks, then wipes at her own. I take the hint and knock three more pieces that were stuck to my face off my cheeks.

A hard pulse thumps in my eyes as I realize the entire class is staring at me. I bet they think I'm going to croak. Just as I catch my breath, Sunny takes it away again by asking a question.

"Is it real? I mean, it's a real slave shack? I wanna see it!"

London blurts out, "Will we get to go inside? Is there still slave stuff in it?"

My blouse is soaked in the back from mist. Is the

air conditioning on? Is anybody else misting?

Then Mrs. Jacobs adds, "I'm happy to hear the enthusiasm, because there *will* be a quiz on what we learn."

That's not enthusiasm she hears; that's joke material they're gathering.

Sunny exaggerates a sigh. "Really, Mrs. Jacobs? A quiz?"

Here come the moans and groans, because now it's *not* just my worst nightmare field trip, it's my worst nightmare field trip with a graded quiz attached! I can't believe that woman fixed her lips to invite everybody to see my shame. She just handed out permission slips like they were movie tickets for admission to *Laura Dyson's Lowdown, Dirty, Backwoods Family Secret!*

Then I remember the most important person ever. Oh, no.

I shift my attention to the right. Troy's glaring at me, and I notice his baseball cards have fallen from his lap onto the floor. Maybe he's as shocked as I am, but I've got to get this situation under control before it gets out of hand. So I just blurt out what I'm thinking.

"It's not really a slave shack. It's just . . . a . . . really old . . . little house. Come on! You guys are going to make me ding you!"

The bell rings and I pop out of that tight desk like a muffin in a toaster. I don't want to talk to anybody.

I've got to get out of here. My pants are making that *weeshy-sweeshy* noise as I rush down the hall, but right now I don't care. The way I see it, I've only got two choices. Either figure out a way to get rid of that shack or make sure the field trip never happens. Because even though I hate coming to school right now, my life is cake and ice cream compared to the torment I'll take from my classmates if they set their eyes on that shack.

chapter ten

I make my way to bus 189 for my first trip back to the farm. My ankles just stopped throbbing from that long morning walk, and now I've got a matching pain in my head.

I climb the steps and take a seat toward the back of the bus. Soon, Sage makes her way down the aisle to join me. It's not until Sage bends to sit that I see Sunny behind her. She takes a seat on the other side and picks at me right away.

"So, Laura, I'm kind of floored by what I learned in history class today. That's a pretty big secret you've been keeping."

I don't respond. I refuse to look at her. Troy and Shane come down the aisle and take the seat in front of us as Sunny keeps talking.

"I can't believe your family still has a slave shack on their property."

Neither can I. Sage's shoulders rise toward her ears. Her face is still but her eyes are ping-ponging back and forth from Sunny to me as Sunny keeps talking.

"I mean, it seems creepy that an African American family would have a slave shack in their yard. I'm just trying to get my head around that."

Me, too, but I wish she'd put a cork in her mouth and shut up. Then she talks crazy. "So does this mean your family owned slaves?"

I yell at her. "Heck to the tenth power of no way!"

Sage turns to me. "I didn't tell, Laura. I swear."

I'm fighting mad. "I know. Don't worry, Sage. I got this."

My brain blanks and leaves me scrambling for a response. Suddenly I get an idea about how to downgrade the situation.

"There's no slave shack, Sunny. Mrs. Jacobs has us confused with somebody else. You know how old people get things mixed up."

Troy turns and stares at me. "Really?"

But Sunny won't let it go. "Mrs. Jacobs has never been wrong about stuff like this before. I mean, why would she lie? And anyway, I'd believe a teacher before I'd believe you."

She stands and smiles at Sage. "Leaving."

Sage brightens up. "Yeah, okay!"

After Sunny leaves, Sage whispers, "That was weird."

I'm focused on Sunny's back as she walks toward the front. Maybe if I focus hard enough, she'll trip and smash her face on the floor. Sage takes a pad of paper and a pencil from her backpack, shows them to me, and pretends to write. I understand and nod. So she writes:

How did Sunny find out about the shack?

I write back.

Mrs. Jacobs told the whole class. She set up a field trip. I'm so mad.

OMG! What are you going to do?

IDK. Maybe get it canceled. I think my grandma's in on this, too. I'm just so overdone about the whole thing.

Can't believe this is happening. I know you hate the shack, so I hate it, too.

xoxo Thanks, Sage.

I stare out the window, wishing I could magically lift that shack and throw it back into the 1800s where it came from. It's ridiculous to have something so cruel and ugly still standing in the 2000s. I'm deep in my hate fest when Sage nudges me.

"Anyway, I'm covering the baseball game tomorrow. Are you coming?"

I've had that opening-day game marked on my calendar since I found out Troy made the team. Other than Major League Baseball opening day, this was the one game I refused to miss. But I don't want to ruin it for him either. What if I become a distraction with a bunch of lamebrain people like Sunny asking questions about the shack? She'll get loud, and it could mess him up on the mound.

And I'd never forgive myself for that.

I shrug. "I totally planned on going before my parents dropped me off to stay with Grandma. But now I can't."

"That's too bad, Laura."

Sage is still going on and on about the game, so I reach inside my backpack and find my lip gloss and compact. As I'm redoing my lips, Troy throws an imaginary pitch and I forget about Sage.

He gives Shane a high-five, then pounds his fist into his palm.

"Tomorrow's game day! First game of the season,

and I'm on the bump. I'm going to rock and fire, bro. Hey, check it out! We may go undefeated!"

Shane wipes his hand across his messy blond hair, twists the cap off of his drink, raises the plastic bottle to his mouth, then steps on Troy's dream before taking a chug.

"You can forget that. We won't win half. Face it, Troy. You and me are the best they've got, and even with us, our team's not that good. Anyway, let's talk pitches. I think your first three pitches should be fastball, changeup, changeup."

I'm still hot with Sunny for putting me on blast about the shack, but I can't help but hear Troy and Shane's baseball conversation. And without thinking, I slam Shane for his pitch-order suggestions.

"Are you pitching the ball or serving it up for dinner? Why in the world would you throw back-to-back changeups? You throw that to a good batter and he's going yard off you. Who taught you pitching strategies, the scarecrow from *The Wizard of Oz*? Seriously, Shane, if you only had a brain."

Sage giggles. I dig in my backpack for some gum. As I unwrap it, I look up and notice Troy and Shane are in my face.

I pop the gum into my mouth and chew. "What?"

They keep staring, like I'm speaking some kind of mixed-up language like Germ-lish or Span-talian.

Troy finally grins.

"You know baseball?"

I feel Sage glaring at me, but Troy's talking to me in front of the whole bus! And then I realize it might be the worst thing ever if he thinks I'm a freak because I know baseball. Even though I'd love to share with him everything I know about pitching, maybe I shouldn't. He may not like girls who play baseball. So I shake my head and look away.

"No. I just . . . I don't know."

Shane interrupts. "Exactly, Larda. Of course you don't know. Girls don't play baseball, so why are you all in our conversation?"

I'm ready to snatch his plastic bottle and shove it up his nose when Troy grabs the bar on the back of his seat and punches Shane in the arm. "Chillax, bro. A ball player's a ball player. You're right, Larda. Fastball, changeup, changeup isn't a good idea. But how did *you* know?"

I straighten him out. "My name is Laura, not Larda. Anyway, my dad was a patcher in college, so he knows kitches . . . wait, I meant . . ."

Troy frowns. "A what?"

If I could get the window down on this bus, I'd jump.

"I meant to say my dad was a catcher in college, so he knows pitches."

Shane's sticking his finger down his throat and pretending to barf. But Troy just shrugs.

"Your dad played college ball? Sweet!"

Shane sighs. "Just because your dad wore catcher's gear in college doesn't mean he was any good. And it doesn't make *you* an expert."

I roll my neck and lift my palm toward him. "Maybe not, unless you consider First Team All-American, All-Conference, Defensive Player of the Year and two years in the Phillies minor league system good. So talk to the hand because my brain won't understand."

Troy chuckles until he sees Shane's frowning face. That's when I hear Shane whisper, "Now she's double creepy. I can't even believe you're talking to her."

Silence.

Shane flicks Troy on his ear. "Hey, why don't you come over later? We can get an extra practice in before the game tomorrow."

Troy flicks him back. "Can't. I gotta help Dad with his lawn and garden stuff today. We've got a few customers needing service."

I know Troy's dad owns the Home and Garden Store at the corner of Main and Jensen Avenue. It's cool that Troy helps him. But it's even cooler that he talked to me! About baseball!

Sage nudges and I nudge her back. She shows me

the pen and paper again, but this time I shake my head. For the first time in months, even if I *had* an Almond Joy, I couldn't eat it. My stomach's *goink*ing about something else now, and I bet there's little Troy-faced butterflies tickling my insides as I try to control my excitement.

Sage keeps nudging me, but I just want her to leave me alone until the butterflies stop swarming.

When the bus stops near her house, she gets up and plasters a megagrin across her face.

"Bye, Laura. See you tomorrow. You can call me if you want to talk about . . ." Sage cuts her eyes to the back of Troy's head, then back to me. ". . . you know."

I'm sure my grin looks like hers. "Bye, Sage."

Once the bus is empty, I'm left alone to relive the conversation over and over again, but the good feelings don't last long. Shack drama is making itself top priority in my mind. I've got to put an end to this field trip thing. I don't have any choice, because I can't take a chance on Troy, Sunny, or any of my classmates seeing the shack.

Heck to the hundredth power of no way.

chapter eleven

I open the screen door. "Grandma? Where are you?"

"In the living room!"

I rush in and find her with a book in her hand and a baseball game on the television. I walk slowly to her chair and look at her face.

"Were you asleep?"

She's flipping pages with a frown. "I don't understand why the right-handed batters are so happy that the new pitcher is left-handed. I can't find an answer in my book."

Finally she looks up at me and smiles. "But I did learn that a steal is just a runner going from one base to another while a batter is at the plate. Not the kind of thief I was thinking of."

My jaw drops as I read the cover. *Learn Everything You Need to Know About Baseball in Two Hours or Less.* What the what?

"How was your day, Baby Girl?"

That question brings me back to the shack drama. Even though the Chicago Cubs are playing the Milwaukee Brewers, I can't get into that right now.

"Grandma, you got a minute? We need to talk."

She presses the mute button on the remote and closes her book.

"What's wrong?"

I'm pacing. "Everything. Mrs. Jacobs gave out permission slips for my class to visit the shack. Did you set that up, Grandma?"

She grins. "Surprise!" But as she looks at me, her smile fades. "You don't have to go into the shack if you're not ready. It's different for you than it is for the other children. I understand."

I take deep breaths and let them out slowly. I even count to ten in my mind before saying anything.

"No, Grandma. That's not it. See, I don't want my classmates in there, either. I'm not proud of the shack. It's a terrible, terrible place. I'm sure awful things happened in there to our ancestors. Besides that, this stuff is so yesterday's news. And yesterday's history."

She points at me. "Exactly. Yesterday is history, and if you don't learn from what happened yesterday, you'll never get things right today or even have a chance to get them right tomorrow. Understand?"

"Yes, I get it, but . . ."

Grandma cuts me off. "No buts, Laura Eboni. There's lots of history in the shack, history that will have a direct impact on your life. It's yours to use or not use. But you don't have the right to stop others from using it."

"So you're saying you'll let me be the laughingstock of my entire school? I mean, my classmates know what kind of brutal things happened during slavery. They also know cruel stuff happened inside slave shacks. And they'll look at me like I'm crazy for keeping one. It's as if we don't care about how our ancestors were treated."

Grandma stands. "You don't know the whole story, Baby Girl. It's time to be proud of who you are."

I plop down on the couch. "I can't be proud of something my ancestors were forced to live through. Disgusting things went on in there! I don't understand why you can't see how terrible that makes us look! We might as well have the whips and shackles on display! Are those inside the shack, too? It was an unbelievably bad time in the lives of African Americans, Grandma! We need to move on."

Grandma sits down and holds up her book. "You heard all the stuff I said at the ballpark last night, didn't you?"

"Yes."

"That's because *I* didn't get it. I just considered baseball a dumb sport that grown people played when they should be out looking for a *real* job. But after seeing how much you love the game, I'm doing my best to understand it."

I look back at the television as the pitcher throws a strike, and Grandma starts up again.

"And I'm not doing this just because you're my granddaughter. I'm learning about baseball because that's what the women in the Laura Line would do. We're connected through blood but united by choice. Whether you like it or not, Baby Girl, you're part of the Line."

I've heard enough. "Grandma, I'm going outside for a while, okay?"

"I hope you're not mad at me."

I shake my head because I don't feel like talking anymore. Instead, I go to my room and put on a pair of sweatpants and an old T-shirt Dad gave me that was too small for him. I lace up my black Converse high-tops, slap a ball cap on my head, step outside, and tromp across the grass.

All this talk about trying and promises and doing

my best is too hard. My parents want me to live in a place I totally hate but they act like it's better than Disney World. I know there's not this much drama in the Magic Kingdom.

First, I can't believe Grandma just set up the worst field trip ever for my history class without talking to me about it, and now, even though she knows how I feel about the field trip, she refuses to cancel it.

Second, Sage is getting played like a clarinet and can't see it. The more I point it out, the angrier she gets at me. She's dying for popularity, especially since she hasn't had it since third grade, before we got tagged as fat girls.

I don't need this.

There's only one thing I *need* to do right now, and I'm on my way to do it. I reach the pitching area Dad set up for me and grab my glove off the top of the bucket of baseballs. I don't have much time left before it'll be dark, so I drag the bucket closer to my pitcher's mound, pick up a baseball, and get started.

Holding that little white ball with red laces in my hand takes me back to the last time I pitched to Dad. The pain returns, so I throw five straight heaters at the glove nailed to the tree above home plate.

BLAM . . . BLAM . . . BLAM . . . BLAM . . . BLAM.

I should've warmed up first, but since Dad's not

here to make me, I didn't. Besides, I'm pretty warm inside already. Now that I know Grandma's not going to cancel the field trip, I'll have to work alone on getting that done. Or maybe I can force the shack to be temporarily closed. Yeah. Now there's an idea.

BLAM . . . BLAM . . . BLAM.

I'll get Sage to help me. She's great at figuring things out. Well, except I haven't really helped her with that Pink Chip invitation. How could Sage think I was jealous? Those girls are snakes! Just the thought of something slithering near my feet makes me check the ground before picking up three more baseballs.

BLAM . . . BLAM . . . BLAM.

And seriously, I have no intention of helping Sage become a Pink Chip. Heck to the double no. I'll have to make her see my point. No matter what it takes.

BLAM . . . BLAM . . . BLAM . . . BLAM.

My arm's hurting. Maybe I *should've* warmed up. I try to shake the pain away, but it's not working. So I gather the baseballs and put them back in the bucket, drop my glove on top, and head to Grandma's house. Before I open the door, I can hear Grandma inside.

"He was safe! That second baseman missed the tag! He's not out! Hey, umpire, you need glasses. Here, you can borrow mine!"

I wait before opening the screen door. Mom's face appears in my mind. I promised her I would try my best, and I am. But Grandma's making it so hard. How can I go in there and pretend nothing's wrong? I know. I'll pretend I'm at school and just say nothing.

The television announcer is talking as loud as Grandma.

"Well, folks, he clearly missed that call."

Grandma agrees. "Ya doggone skippy he did! That umpire can't see doodly-squat!"

I wonder if all old people talk like that. But what's really weird is . . . I understand her. When she sees me, she points to the television. "Baby Girl, I read in the book that if a guy is on a base, and he runs to the next base to steal, the infielder has to tag him in order for him to be out. Is that right?"

I nod and watch the replay. No doubt. The guy was safe.

Grandma leans back in her chair. "Then the umpires are cheating. They called that boy out, and I could see he was safe from here. That just burns my buns. Come sit down and watch the game with me. I'm beginning to catch on, and tomorrow, I'm going to try and keep score!"

What the what? She's been reading and watching baseball for one day, and the look on her face tells me that I might have to make my own dinner tonight. Suddenly, the coach comes out of the dugout and starts screaming at the umpire. Grandma picks up what's happening.

"Well, it's about time somebody came to take up for that boy. He was safe."

After just a moment of arguing, the umpire points over the stadium seats and the crowd goes crazy.

Grandma's flipping through pages. "What just happened?"

I step closer to the television and jab my hands on my hips, then hold them straight out in the air.

"He got tossed! The umpire kicked him out of the park."

Grandma's furious. "For what, telling the truth?"

Then she leans back and sighs. "Well, now I know of *two* things that'll get you kicked out of a ballpark."

I don't want to laugh, but I can't help it as I think about those pork chop sandwiches. When I look her way, she's got the cutest grin on her face, and there's no way I can be mad at her.

"Looks like you're really getting into baseball, Grandma."

She nods. "And I never would've known if I hadn't tried."

The only sound in the room is coming from the television. I know she's trying to throw me a message about the shack—I'm just not trying to catch it. She reaches in her blouse again, and I step back. She pulls out a twenty-dollar bill and I exhale.

"Order us a big pizza, Laura. I didn't get around to cooking anything. The number for Pug's Pizza Palace is on the refrigerator."

I order our pizza, and we demolish it while watching the game. When it's over, I shuffle off to my room to finish my science and English homework. Digging through my backpack, I accidentally pull out my permission slip for the field trip. I stare at it like it's my number-one enemy, ball it up, and stuff it in the desk drawer.

Even though it's just a piece of paper, to me it's giving free access to a terrible time in my family's history. It's hard enough to take the cruel jokes about my weight. But if jokes are made about whatever's inside that shack, it may hurt even more than being called Fat Larda, because what they say about me is one thing. What they say about my family or our property is fighting words.

And I can't get suspended from school for fighting, especially over something as ridiculous as that ugly shack.

That settles it. I'll have to handle this myself.

chapter twelve

Yesterday, Mrs. Jacobs stopped me in the hall before school started. Today, I'm looking for her. There she is, on her way to the teachers' break room.

"Mrs. Jacobs!"

She turns around and waits for me. "Good morning, Laura. Everything okay?"

My heart's pumping double beats, but I've got to get this off my chest. I look behind me, hoping no one notices I'm hanging out with a teacher.

"Can we talk in private somewhere?"

She looks around and points to the band room. "Sure. Let's go in there."

Once we're inside, I close the door, take a breath, get my serious face on, and unload.

"I'd like to talk to you about the field trip."

She grins. "Are you excited?"

I keep the serious face working. "I think you should cancel it."

The edges of her grin straighten and the mood immediately changes to uneasy. I grab the ends of my pigtails and twist them as Mrs. Jacobs crosses her arms.

"I thought you'd be thrilled, since it would put a spotlight on your ancestors."

I look away. "Mrs. Jacobs, please don't be mad at me, but I don't want my classmates visiting the shack. If they see it, I'll be the laughingstock of the whole school."

Her head tilts to the side. "What do you mean? Didn't you hear the excitement in class when I made the announcement?"

"You heard excitement. I heard jokes. I mean, it's one thing to study slavery in class, but now you're making it personal. In case you don't know, I'm not the most popular girl in school, and the field trip is just going to make things worse. They're going to laugh at me, Mrs. Jacobs. Everybody's going to laugh."

She's got a spacey look on her face, and I know she doesn't get what I'm saying. I fight the urge to cry because I'm so tired of being made fun of. I hate the fat jokes and the dumb names. And just like my classmates are mean, I think mean things happened in that shack to my ancestors. So eventually the fat jokes will turn into slave jokes, and the dumb names will turn to names like Fat Shack Larda if I don't get this canceled.

"Mrs. Jacobs, I just want to be . . . normal."

She puts her hand on my shoulder. "I don't know if you'll ever be normal, Laura. And I say that as a good thing."

The warning bell rings, and we both look out the small window in the door as students scramble toward class. Mrs. Jacobs switches her stuff back to the other arm.

"Tell you what—let's talk more about it after class today. How's that?"

I nod, open the door, and leave. What a waste of time. I'm not talking to her after class. Heck to the double no.

I'm cautious going down the hall, expecting a bunch of jokes about the field trip. But no one says a word about it. All they talk about is today's baseball game. But during history, things get out of hand. Sunny is the first to irritate me.

"So Laura, did you find the shack Mrs. Jacobs was talking about?"

I ignore her, take my seat, open my history book, and try to look busy. She's got four of our classmates with her, and they're giggling as she continues.

"You don't have anybody still living in that thing, do you?"

I roll my eyes. "Why? Are you looking for a new home?"

There are chuckles all around me as more classmates gather at my desk. Sunny frowns. "You're the one with the slave shack, Laura. And you're too ashamed to admit it."

I snap at her. "You don't know anything about me!"

"Then why'd you lie about it on the bus yesterday?"

The crowd goes silent. All I see are eyes zooming in on me. I'm trapped, and Sunny knows it. Then Mrs. Jacobs walks in and closes the door.

"Please take your seats so we can begin."

Sunny gives me a long, evil glare before walking back to her desk. What am I going to do? She called me out, and I've got to come up with a good reason for lying. I look through my history book and pretend to read as Mrs. Jacobs talks. On one page I see a picture of men signing the Declaration of Independence. On the next page a king and queen seem happy with all their servants around them.

Wait. That's it!

I close my history book and move around in my seat until I can see Troy. I sure hope Sunny asks about the shack again, because I've got an answer for her.

And when the bell rings, I get my wish.

I slide out of my desk and take my time gathering my stuff, trying to give Sunny an opportunity to reach me. She comes with a crowd, but when Troy eases over and joins the group, my brain fogs and I bite my lip to focus. Sunny goes straight for the knockout.

"So back to the question I asked before class. Why'd you lie, Larda?"

"Wait a minute." I jam my left hand on my left hip and shift all of my weight to my left leg. Whether or not I'm lying is no longer the issue. It's a war of words between me and the Pink Chip princess, and nobody's ever had enough guts to take her on.

Until now.

My right pointer finger shakes back and forth in her face as I tell her what's on my mind.

"You must have me confused with one of those potato chips you hang out with."

She corrects me. "Pink Chips."

I roll my eyes. "Whatever. An-y-way, you need to be careful who you call a liar. I didn't lie. It really isn't a slave shack. It's a storage shed, full of important documents and . . . and things . . . antique stuff worth thousands of dollars. And the last thing I want is a bunch of wannabe-important, grubby-handed haters touching our stuff or, worse, trying to steal it."

Sunny shakes her head to get her bangs out of her face and frowns. "Are you calling me a thief, Larda? You owe me an apology."

I don't have any bangs, so I rub my hand across my hair to smooth it down, then match her look. "And you'll get one right after you apologize for calling me a liar, Sunny."

A few in the crowd chuckle as Sunny turns cloudy. I hear Troy whisper to someone, "I can't believe Larda said that to Sunny!"

Mrs. Jacobs calls from her desk, "Is everything okay back there?"

I'm dead red on Sunny. "Everything's fine, Mrs. Jacobs."

Then Mrs. Jacobs looks my way. "Laura, did you still want to talk about the field trip?"

Her timing couldn't have been worse. I need her to leave or I could really lose this war.

"Not right now, Mrs. Jacobs. I'll talk with you later."

"Okay, just let me know. I have some ideas you might like."

I rush through the crowd and out into the hall. Sunny and a few others follow me. I get to my locker and open it. If she wants to go head up with me, then

I'm down. As I get my stuff to go home, I push Sunny's button one more time.

"Are you here to apologize? If not, you need to bounce."

Sunny grins. "I'll want to check out this 'storage shed' for myself . . . before the field trip."

I cut her off. "Heck to the triple no you won't!"

But she keeps going. "And if I'm wrong, then I'll apologize to you in front of the entire class. But if you refuse to let me go in before the field trip, then you'll be known as Fat Larda, the big fat liar."

There's a hush in the crowd. All eyes zoom in like spotlights. Blood whooshes through me, and my heart pounds so hard, my whole body thumps. I blink away tears, but soon there's mist on my arms, as if those tears were determined to find a way out. I slam my locker closed and rush by Sunny and her friends without a comeback. The only thing I can think of to say is really lame, but I say it anyway.

"I'll think about it."

I'm on the move. I don't want to stand around so they can see the shock in my face. I'm rushing down the hall, eyes as big as headlights. What did I just do?

Sage calls out to me as she stands next to a stack of school newspapers. "Don't forget I'm covering the baseball game today. Laura? Laura?"

I wave before turning the corner. The bus leaves

soon, and I didn't even get a chance to wish Troy good luck in his game. I wanted to tell him to make sure he never throws fastball, changeup, changeup, no matter what Shane says.

Maybe I could have given him some pointers, like inhale on your windup and exhale on the throw. I mean, he talked to me yesterday, didn't he? *A ball player's a ball player.* That's what he said on the bus.

But no. Here I am, rushing to get away from Sunny instead of wishing my Hunky Chunky the best game of his life. And it's all because of the shack. I was too busy defending it, and now I've got to defend myself.

When the bus stops in front of Grandma's mailbox, I step off and wait for the bus to roll away before I start my hike down the gravel road. I'm kicking more rocks than I step on. The little pebbles dig into the bottoms of my shoes, and it's almost like walking in sand. I can't get a good stride, and I hate all the noise I'm making with each step.

CRUNCH, CRUNCH, CRUNCH.

That's how Sunny made me feel today.

CRUNCH, CRUNCH, CRUNCH.

My cell phone's vibrating my backpack. I stop and answer it while I check the road for snakes. The caller ID shows Larry Dyson.

"Dad! Hello?"

"Hey! How's my little pitcher doing?"

I exhale. "I'm . . . okay, really. How's Mom?"

"She's right here, trying to take the phone from me. Hold on."

I hear chuckles, and that makes me feel better, knowing that they're not all tight and tense. Suddenly, Mom's soft voice drifts into my ear.

"Laura?"

My face twists, and I bite my lip to control what I say and how I say it. I don't want her to know I've got drama. She calls to me again.

"Are you there?"

I hesitate before answering. "I'm here."

There's a quiet between us that tells me I've probably set her knower in motion. I hear Dad in the background questioning her. I bet her smile faded.

"What's wrong?"

"Nothing, Mom."

Silence.

"Laura Eboni, if you don't talk to me, I'm going to worry until you do."

I can't hate on her knower, because usually it's on point, just like it is right now.

As I open my mouth to speak, it's as if my throat has narrowed, only allowing so much of my drama to come out. But I think it's the biggest piece.

"Grandma and Mrs. Jacobs planned a field trip to the shack for my history class without telling me about it. I don't want the field trip to happen, Mom. And they won't cancel it. I mean . . . my classmates already make fun of me. And now I'm never going to live down the fact that we have a slave shack on our property."

Silence.

I'm waiting for Mom to say something, and when she does, her voice is on high volume, and I wish I had kept the whole situation to myself.

"Then put all of your energy into getting that field trip canceled. Even though you've never gone inside to see what the shack is all about, nobody else should have that opportunity either. Don't you agree?"

Mom only uses that voice and tone when she's being sarcastic. She's got me all wrong.

"That's not what I said, Mom."

"It's exactly what you're saying."

"So you think just because I'm the only person who doesn't want the field trip to happen, that makes me wrong?"

Mom sighs. "No, but it's exactly what your classmates are doing to you. They see a young girl who happens to be bigger, and they judge her based on what she looks like on the outside, not what's overflowing on the inside. You have a major opportunity here."

I take a step and the crunch makes me think of

what Mom just did to me. She crunched me using my life! How can she compare me to the shack?

I sniffle, wipe my face, and exhale. "Mom, I gotta go."

"Okay, but hold on a minute. Your Dad needs to say something to you. But before I go, I want you to know I love you so much, okay?"

"I love you, too."

There's a short quiet before Dad gets on the phone.

"Laura, I don't know what's going on, but by the look on your mother's face, you've got a situation. Am I right?"

"A big situation, Dad. What am I supposed to do?"

I'm expecting another lecture, but instead he just says two words.

"Go throw."

chapter thirteen

The orchestra's sitting on clouds above my head playing music they created for this special moment. Troy's running in slow motion toward me, and I toward him, through a baseball field of yellow daisies. The closer we get to each other, the louder the music plays above us. Now angels have joined the orchestra with their harps. Troy's arms stretch out for me and mine to him. I pooch my lips and prepare for my first kiss.

KA-BLAM!

I lie on the floor, still dreaming that we're running together through the daisies as the alarm clock gets louder and louder. I open my eyes and stare at my shoes under the bed.

I sit up and look around the room. No orchestra. No daisies. No Troy.

Grandma calls to me from the kitchen. "Baby Girl, are you okay?"

"I'm okay. I'll be out in a minute."

I've never fallen out of bed before. The floor's cold, but I don't mind. Sitting here is still better than going to school today. But I would like to know how Troy did in his game yesterday. I hope he won.

"Laura, you better hurry! Your breakfast is getting cold."

Can't be any colder than this floor. But I get up, zip through the shower, get dressed, eat breakfast, and head out. With only twelve minutes before the bus comes, I up the pace and pay the price for it when I'm all out of breath at the bus stop.

Even though I'm huffing and puffing, I pull out my mirror and check my makeup. I don't want to look like one of those Picasso paintings, all melted and swirled into a mess of something to make you scream.

By the time the bus pulls up, I'm back on my game, breathing steady and looking great. I sit in the same spot, near the back, right where Troy spoke to me yesterday. When he gets on the bus, I open my mouth to speak, but he walks by as if I weren't there.

Did he just ignore me? He shuffles to the last seat in the back row. I turn around to check on him. He's still frowning, with his arms crossed over his chest.

When Shane gets on the bus, he sits in the front, and I now know something really bad has happened. Sage sits next to me, and I nod toward the back seats.

"What's up with him? This bus has been creepy quiet and nobody's sitting near Troy."

She shrugs. "They lost their opener. Troy pitched and Shane caught. Between Troy throwing the worst pitches ever and Shane being the worst catcher ever, they looked like Pee-Wee Little Leaguers. It was pathetic and embarrassing."

I glance over my shoulder at Troy. His head's down. "I feel so bad for him."

Sage grins. "Sunny, London, and Amanda were there, getting all kinds of attention. Even guys from the other team were trying to get their names and digits. I took pictures of Sunny rooting for our team. And then the most awesome thing happened."

I'm scared to ask, so I just look at her, which proves to be enough.

"Sunny asked me if I was still interested in joining. I said yes. She told me they'd be in contact about initiation and I said, 'No problem.' How cool is that?"

I don't say anything, because to me, it's not cool at all. When the bus driver pulls to the curb and stops, we get up and form a line in the aisle. Sage whispers over her shoulder.

"But the Pink Chips were really talking about Troy in a bad way."

I grimace. "What did they say?"

We step off of the bus and head toward school as Sage answers me.

"Just stuff about him not being a very good pitcher and how he wasn't representing the Blue Chips."

I frown. "If Sunny wants to talk about *stuff*, she should start with how much bogus *stuff* flies out of that mouth of hers."

Sage looks to see if Sunny heard me, then frowns. "Loosen up, Laura. It's just her opinion. I'm going to fix my hair. You coming?"

I shake my head. "See you at lunch."

My mind drifts to Troy. No wonder he's not very talkative this morning. Shane needs to learn how to catch the ball. I bet most of that loss was his fault.

I grab my first-, second-, and third-period books from the locker, and just as I'm about to load them into my backpack, I hear Sage calling me.

"Laura! Wait!"

Her eyes look wild. "Guess what I just heard! The Pink Chips put Troy on Blue Chip probation with one strike. And unlike baseball, Pink Chips say two strikes and you're out."

My backpack slides from my fingers. "The Pink Chips control the Blue Chips, too?"

Sage whispers, "Yes. They decide which guys stay and which ones get the boot."

I can't believe it. "So Troy's on boot alert because of one bad game?"

Sage shrugs. "They said he didn't represent. I thought you should know. One more bad day on the mound, and Troy's going to be yesterday's Blue Chip. And from what I've heard, it's better to have never been a Pink or Blue Chip than to get booted. Gotta run. If I hear anything else, I'll tell you at lunch."

The cafeteria feels overcrowded. I don't know why I'm feeling cramped but I am. Sage is going on and on about how she needs a new outfit before her initiation into the Pink Chips when a low murmur makes me look around to see what's happening.

It's them.

Across the room Sunny leads her entourage through the cafeteria table maze, walking so slowly that it makes me sleepy. Amanda and London sashay behind her. They don't look at any of us, but all eyes are definitely on them. Their daily walk never seems to lose its draw. But I've got my own take.

To me, Sunny's name should have been Tsunami, because she doesn't make people smile like a sunny day does. But she's excellent at ruining people's lives, just like a tsunami does. She smiles at Sage as she passes our table, and Sage speaks as if Sunny just cast a spell on her.

"Cute dress, Sunny. How's it going? See you later!"

Troy's at the table with his baseball buddies. They don't seem to be upset with him about yesterday's loss. Actually, they're all talking and bumping fists with him. Just as the Pink Chips pass their table, Shane Doyles calls out, "Sunny, Sunny, won't you be my honey? I'll even give you money!"

Sunny ignores him. Shane's not a Blue Chip, so he's just as ignorable as the rest of us. Even though most of the guys are cracking up, Troy's not laughing. He's glaring at Sunny.

Amanda is the second most popular Pink Chip. She's so thin I could use her to pick the coconut out of my teeth after my Almond Joy moments. Her skin is a beautiful brown and as smooth as my Almond Joy, minus the nut. But her microbraids set everything off, especially when she wears her pink jeans, black sweater, and black pumps. I have to give her props. She's catwalk ready and I can't hate on her.

But if I had to pick a favorite Pink Chip, it would be London. She's the only Pink Chip with bright red hair and freckles. Maybe it's the green eyes that make her stand out. Even though pink clashes with her hair, she wears it, because Pink Chips have to wear something pink every day.

London gives Sage hope because back in sixth grade London was called Raggedy Ann, like that homely freckle-faced doll. She was even more unpopular than Sage is now. But when we got to middle school, things changed for London.

And I mean everything got better.

She cut her hair into this cute little bob that surrounded her face and accented those amazing green eyes. Then she changed her wardrobe from drab to fab, wearing black vests over her pink tops, fingerless black gloves, and bangin' black ankle boots.

She worked hard to become a Pink Chip, and it paid off. Nobody calls her Raggedy Ann anymore. I glance at my best friend. She knows London's story, and I bet she's counting on being another chapter in the "unpopular girl turns popular" saga.

I'm happy when the bell rings to end lunch. I'd rather go to fifth period than watch that dumb Pink Chip parade.

After working in the office, I rush to history class like I always do. Except today, when I speak to Troy he doesn't speak back. He sits at his desk and stares out the window. I guess he knows he's on probation and it's bothering him.

I want to give Troy a hug, tell him everything is

okay. But since I'm Fat Larda, that would only make things worse for him.

And I guess it's brutal to the tenth power that Sunny's sitting next to him. She's the one who put him on probation—I'm sure of it. I could just walk up there and smack all the air out of her lungs. Soon, there's a knock on the door, and Mrs. Jacobs answers it. It's an office worker with a yellow slip. Mrs. Jacobs looks toward the other side of the room.

"Troy, you're wanted in the office."

He gets up and leaves. Dang, that boy is fine. Now that he's gone, I don't have anybody to stare at. I wonder if his dad has left him the key again. The other day in the hall, he told me he was picking up the house key. And what's up with that? I mean, is he forgetful or something? I'm all in Troy's business when Mrs. Jacobs snaps my concentration.

"I'm still waiting for a few permission slips. Please get those back to me as soon as possible. And Laura, I'd like to speak with you after class for a moment, so please don't leave."

I nod and immediately open my history book to avoid all the stares that I know I'm getting even though I'm not looking up to actually see them. One part of my forehead feels warm, and I think that must be the spot Sunny's staring at.

When the bell rings, I sit still and wait for the

classroom to empty. Mrs. Jacobs strolls down the aisle and sits at the desk across from me.

"Let's finish our conversation. And if you miss your bus, it's okay. I'll take you home."

Oh heck to the double no she won't! Being seen with a teacher outside of school is an automatic diagnosis of Teacher's Pet Disorder, and that's the last thing I need.

So I get to the point. "Are you thinking about canceling the field trip?"

She shakes her head. "You haven't been in the shack yet, have you?"

I feel as though someone shone a light in my face. "Why would you ask me that?"

She shrugs. "It's obvious. If you had, we wouldn't be having these secret conversations."

Is she trying to use psychology on me? I get up, strap on my backpack, and head to the door.

"Mrs. Jacobs, the shack is wrong, and going inside won't make it right. Slaves were forced to live there. Now you're trying to force me to go in it, too. And I'm not going to do it."

chapter fourteen

Dad would be so proud of me. I've thrown every day since he's been gone. Not because I just wanted to throw, but because the drama in my life is so strong that I can only relieve my mind with pitching.

And today is no different.

I open the screen door and spot a meat loaf cooling on the kitchen counter. There's a bowl of green beans next to it. On the table is the yummiest-looking pasta salad with those squiggly, telephone-cord-shaped pasta pieces, black olives, tomatoes, and little squares of cheese.

I stroll into the living room and find Grandma asleep with the baseball book in her lap and another day game playing on the tube. She's really getting into this baseball thing. It's almost scary how she just took to it like it was a part of her that's been missing. I tiptoe away without waking her.

In my room, I put on my sweats, get my earbuds, and wrap them around my neck. I grab my iPod Nano and clip it to my sweatpants. Sometimes I like to throw pitches in silence. But not today. I want the volume pumped up and rattling every part of me as I throw gas at Dad's glove.

Outside, I grab the handle on my bucket of baseballs and carry them to my pitcher's mound. When Dad's face appears in my mind, I know what he wants me to do. I put the bucket down, lean against a tree, and stretch. As I pull my arm across my body, I think about how much I miss him.

I turn up the music and let Beyoncé change my mood and relax my mind. I wrap my fingers across the red laces and stare down my target. Then I zing a fastball over the square and into Dad's glove.

POP!

Perfect. Beyoncé's jamming in my ears, and I begin to sing along. I even add a few of the steps from a video I've seen on MTV before I throw two more fastballs.

POP! POP!

Yeah, those were nice. Since I'm feeling as if my life has taken a major curve, I think I'll throw a few of those, just to see if they open up my thoughts. I can't believe how Mrs. Jacobs read me so easily.

POP!

Grandma probably told her I hadn't gone into the shack.

POP!

That curveball was pretty good, but it didn't hit the mitt like I wanted. I throw another one. It cuddles inside Dad's glove for a moment before falling out, and I know, if I were a pitcher, *that* curveball would send batters back to the dugout. I reach into my pocket. I better eat my Almond Joy before it melts. After this one, I'll only have three left, so I don't want it to go to waste. I rip the paper off and hold that almost melted chocolate bar between my lips while I get another ball. It's so hot out here that the chocolate's melting on my mouth. Mmm.

I work my lips to push the candy onto my tongue without using my hand, then chew and dance to the rhythm of the music playing in my ears before throwing another curveball.

POP!

My sweatshirt's wet. I'm misting much more than I thought I would. I lift my elbow and sniff my armpit.

Whew! Suddenly, Sage's favorite song blares through my earbuds.

What am I going to do about Sage? She's in for a huge letdown. But even worse, she thinks I don't support her. But I do! It's Sunny I don't support. She doesn't care about Sage. Sunny cares about Sunny; end of story. I pick up a ball from the bucket to throw a knuckleball, then lift my left elbow to sniff that pit before continuing. While I'm sniffing, my eyes roam between the trees and over near the shack.

That's when I see him and freeze midsniff.

What's he doing here? I put my arm down as Troy eases through the flower bed with a cylinder can connected to a hose, spraying the flowers in front of the shack. There's a shiny green bicycle with the kickstand down not far from where he's spraying. It's the ugliest bike in the galaxy with a big black basket on the side of it.

I've never seen Troy with a blue bandana tied around his head like the one he's sporting now. And he's got a white cloth hanging from the back pocket of his jean shorts, which must be his shirt since he's not wearing one. In my mind, the arrow on his Hunky Chunky meter is spinning out of control.

But as much as I want to be excited about seeing him, I'm just the opposite, because:

1. Troy's working in front of the number-one most embarrassing thing in my life right now, and I didn't have any warning that he'd be here.
2. I'm all misty, and I bet my hair is sticking up all over my head.
3. I may have wet armpit stains.
4. He may have seen me sniffing 'em.

I shuffle toward him, even though I have no idea what I'm going to say when I get there. It's too late to hide the shack, so I've got to act as if it's no big deal. In trying to be cool, I say the lamest thing ever.

"Hey! There's a Blue Chip in the flower garden!"

Troy ignores me. So I go for something normal.

"Whatcha' doin'?"

He keeps spraying. "What does it look like I'm doing?"

"Oh. Is that bug spray?"

"No, it's people spray."

What the what? I've got my hands on my hips now.

"Are you always this rude? I mean, ding, I just asked what you were doing. Since you're going to be all nasty about it, I'll just come right out and ask you: What are you doing here?"

Troy puts his can down, wipes the sweat from his

forehead, and grabs a Gatorade sitting on the shack steps. "Sorry. I've kind of had a bad day. Yeah, I'm working."

He chugs his drink, but I'm confused. "I thought your dad owned the Home and Garden Store on Main and Jensen."

Troy sets his Gatorade back on the step before answering. "He *did*, but the economy got bad or something; I don't really know what happened. Anyway, people stopped buying stuff. So he doesn't own that store anymore. This is what we do."

He reaches into his back pocket and pulls out a business card and gives it to me.

"Bailey and Bailey Lawn and Landscaping. I'm the second Bailey on the card."

I stare at it, then slip it into my pocket. He turns to me and grimaces.

"What were you doing over there?"

I look over my shoulder and realize he can't see my stadium because of the trees. I'm scared to tell him the truth since Shane's already called me double creepy for knowing so much about baseball. But I can't lie either, because Troy and I are standing in front of the biggest lie I've told this year. Oh, I know what I can say!

I smile. "I was just stretching and practicing."

He's staring at my lips, and I'm thinking good

things are about to happen until he bursts my bubble.

"Practicing what? You don't chew tobacco, do you? What's all that dark stuff on your mouth? It looks like you did a face plant into a big pile of . . . Did you fall?"

Silence.

A fly buzzes near my mouth and I swat at it. I forgot about the melted chocolate on my lips. I turn and let my tongue sweep across my mouth like the world's fastest windshield wiper.

I turn back to him, hoping I licked it all off.

He starts spraying again. "So why'd you lie about the shack?"

Dang. He just jumps from one hard question to another. And it's not like I can lie again, especially when he's standing beside the big ugly thing.

I shrug. "Wouldn't you? I mean, I hate it."

His head tilts. "You're part of the Laura Line, aren't you?" Suddenly, a smile spreads across his face, and his dimples wave at me as he talks.

"That ledger's got to be the coolest thing ever."

He drops the spray can and holds up both hands. "No disrespect to the Lauras. I've never touched it, I swear!"

I know he's saying something to me, but my mind isn't anywhere close to this farm. I'm standing at the altar with him, dressed in the prettiest white gown ever, and he's sharper than a two-edged sword in his white tuxedo. Then the minister says, "Is there anyone who believes these two should not marry? Speak now or forever hold your peace."

Troy raises his hand. "I do. She's a liar."

"Laura!"

I fall out of my wedding dress and back into my sweats. "Huh?"

"I'm serious. I've never touched it."

I'm lost. "Touched what?"

"The ledger!"

He's staring at me, waiting for a response, and I don't even know what the what he's talking about. All I know is, I lied and he's cute. And of all the conversations I've imagined having with Troy, I can't believe we're here, having this one. But I answer anyway.

"Oh, right, okay."

Troy nods and keeps talking. "And that graveyard of crosses behind the shack is wicked, isn't it? The Laura Line is eerie and cool at the same time. Every once in a while, when I'm here after the sun goes down, I get creeped out when I look at it, because it's so . . . awesome."

"Did you say awesome?"

Troy leaves the planet as he talks. "Heck yeah! You know, like seeing that big statue of Sam Houston down near Huntsville! Or visiting the Alamo in San Antonio! Or . . ."

I put my hand up. "Stop the madness, Troy. I'm not down with history like you are."

I've passed those crosses a bunch of times but never felt the awesome Troy's talking about. More important, how can I make him forget I'm a liar?

Troy keeps talking about the Lauras. "I can't touch the ledger because Dad said it's sacred. But I heard your grandma talk about Laura Elaine. It almost broke me down, but I'm not wimpy, know what I mean?

Troy sticks out his chest and grimaces like a tough guy.

I nod. "I know what you mean."

He picks up his can and sprays the flowers as he talks.

"Have you told Sage about her? Which Laura is your favorite?"

I try one question at a time. "Why would I tell Sage?"

He looks at me with those puppy brown eyes, and I just want to pat his head and put a collar around his neck that says I BELONG TO LAURA. But I manage to ask the question.

"Let's see . . . Laura Elaine . . . now which one is she?"

He frowns. "Seriously? If you don't know, I'm not telling you."

It's as if a loud alarm wakes me up. "It's not like I can't find out for myself."

He spits in the dirt. "I can't believe you don't know this stuff."

The only thing I know right now is that he knows I lied. I stay quiet, but I think Troy reads my expression, because he drops his spray bottle and glares at me.

"Obviously you've never read the Laura Line ledger. But you've been in the shack, right?"

I cut my eyes to the shack door. "Well, I'm thinking about going . . ."

He folds his arms across his chest. "Unbelievable! This is megahistory in Brooks County and it's on your property and you haven't been inside? That should be a crime."

I know Troy loves history, but I'm not going to let him hate on me without a fight.

"It's a slave shack! I mean, ding! Don't you see how wrong that is?"

He surprises me with a counterattack. "You're the one who's wrong! It's way more than a shack, Larda . . . Laura. And the story of Laura Elaine is good and bad and sad and all that. I can't believe you don't know it. You should ding *yourself*!"

"I'll read it . . . someday."

Troy picks up his Gatorade and finishes it before tossing the bottle in a trash bag.

"It's not like I care. I just can't believe that you haven't checked out the shack. Or that you lied about it."

He puts the sprayer in the basket of his bike, then climbs on as his foot lifts the kickstand. "Anyway, I gotta go. Later . . . Dyson."

As Troy rides that raggedy bike down the hill, I realize I'm standing closer to the shack than I ever have before. Troy made it sound like some kind of fabulous castle. But it's not.

I sit on the bottom of the shack steps and admire the flower garden now that I know Troy helped make it. But the enjoyment doesn't last, because there's one thing I know for sure: I've denied the existence of this shack to all my classmates and directly to Troy and Sunny. But the one person I wanted to impress more than anybody else in the world knew I was a liar all along.

On the bright side, I might show him my stadium next time he comes to spray the garden. I should've shown it to him today. Dang it! Baseball is easy to talk about. I probably know more about the game than he does.

The second subject is scary and a lot more difficult. I know he's been inside. And now he knows I haven't. But he really likes it in there. I look up at the lone window of the shack and can't believe I'm thinking what I'm thinking.

chapter fifteen

After I shower and change clothes, I head to the kitchen, where Grandma's waiting on me for dinner. Even though I've got Troy on my brain, I try to push him to the back of my mind so I don't slip and say something about the shack. Grandma says a blessing; then afterward I go straight for the meat loaf and she starts in about that afternoon's game.

"You sure missed a good baseball match today."

I correct her. "Game, not match, Grandma."

She nods. "I saw those Cubs play again. I'm beginning to recognize some of the players when they come up to bat. But why was there a different pitcher today than yesterday?"

I pretend to throw a pitch. "Gotta rest that throwing arm. Starting pitchers usually have a four- or five-day rest before they pitch again."

Grandma nods. "So they won't hurt themselves; that makes sense. Okay, I get it. How was your day? How's Sage doing? You haven't talked about her much since you've been here."

"She's got big-time drama going on."

I scoop pasta salad onto my plate and tell her about Sage and the Pink Chips.

"You know, Grandma, I don't know what to say to her. She's the best photographer I know. Our school newspaper is lucky to have her because she's so good at that kind of stuff. But she wants to be a Pink Chip because she thinks it will make her popular."

I'm waiting for Grandma to say something grandmotherly like *Don't worry, things will work themselves out*. But what she says makes my toes curl and my eyebrows shoot all the way up my forehead, and I wouldn't be surprised if my pigtails were pointing toward the ceiling.

She puts her elbow on the table and holds her face in her palm. "I wish my mother had lived long enough to meet you. She would have loved you, Laura Eboni. And she would have enjoyed Sage, too. See, my mother was a journalist and loved a good news story."

I stand and look out the window. "Did Troy Bailey call you?"

With a bewildered look, she responds, "No. Why?"

Goose bumps ride my arms and I sit back down. "Never mind. Go ahead and finish telling me about your mom." I pick up my glass of iced tea. "What was she like?"

Grandma slowly rocks side to side before starting. I can tell she's enjoying the memory. I'm taking a big gulp of cold iced tea when Grandma drops a bomb.

"My mother's name was Laura Elaine."

I spew tea across the table and drool it on the end of one of my braids. Grandma grabs a dish towel and helps me wipe the table as I squeeze tea out of my hair.

"Laura Elaine was your mother? I'm sorry, I . . . uh . . . got choked. But please, finish telling me about her."

Grandma sits and returns to that happy place she was in moments ago. "Momma was a beautiful woman. All she ever wanted to be was a news reporter. When I was young, I'd sit in the shack on this little wooden chair my daddy made for me and watch her work. That chair had one leg shorter than the other three, and it wobbled, but I didn't care. As a matter of fact, it's still out there in the shack."

Grandma's way down memory lane, back in her childhood, reliving a special moment, and I refuse to disturb her as she continues talking.

"I'd watch Momma type away on the typewriter her boss gave to her. And to help, I'd sing her songs as she worked. Sometimes she'd stop typing and sing along."

"How old were you?"

"Not too old."

She wipes at her eyes, and we finish eating in silence, maybe out of respect for her mom.

After dinner, Grandma scoots back from the table. "I'm going to wash up these dishes while you finish your homework."

I go to my room, but instead of taking the books out of my backpack, I stroll to the window, pull back the curtain, and stare at the shack. Even after watching Grandma enjoy a memory, I still can't *make* myself like it. But I need to work on that, because Troy's got a big crush on the shack and the Lauras. And I've got a crush on him. I twist the wet end of my braid, thinking about the whole situation.

It would be nice to talk to him about something that only he and I could talk about. And that would be *the only* reason I'd step foot in that shack. I've known Troy since last year and he's barely ever spoken to me. This could change everything.

Maybe I can go inside just long enough to learn one thing about the Laura Line. Maybe I'll go tomorrow, just to find out about Laura Elaine. And that'll get things rolling between us. And after that, maybe I'll show him how to pitch. Then he can show me how good a kisser he is.

I close the curtain, do my homework, and go to bed.

All day Thursday I think about my conversations with Troy and Grandma. In history class I stare at him, but not like I've stared at him before. I'm deep in thought, weighing out whether or not I should do what I swore I'd never do, just for him.

And I've made my decision. Heck to the double yes!

Once the bus drops me off at the mailbox, I walk with purpose down the gravel road, but instead of going all the way up the hill, I take a shortcut. I push down a line of rusty barbed wire fence and step over it. I'm watching and listening for anything and everything that might move. I'm so short of breath from all this walking that I'm hoping there's at least one chair inside the shack besides Grandma's wobbly one. And maybe an oxygen tank. And a glass of iced tea. A sandwich wouldn't hurt my feelings. I won't be mad if it has potato chips on the side.

There's the shack. I exhale without inhaling, which throws my breathing off. My heart pounds my chest as if it wants out before I go in. I don't blame my heart one bit. If it weren't for Troy, I wouldn't go inside either.

And today, as I stand near the front door, it looks so much bigger, darker, scarier, creepier, and uglier than it did yesterday. But I'm sure ghosts and slave zombies only come out of the ground at night, so I better get this over with while the sun's high in the sky. There's no such thing as daytime monsters, right?

I order every ounce of courage I have to my legs, look over my shoulder, and see my bedroom window. Soon, I'll be looking out from it, thinking about this very moment. With every step my legs wobble, my body shakes, and I feel like I'm going to puke. I wonder if this is how my ancestors felt when they were forced to live in there.

But of all the things I feel, the one thing that I don't feel is what bothers me the most.

My knower. It's not warning me or doing anything to make me change my mind. So I climb the two steps, turn the dull gray doorknob, and push. The door whines as I ease my head inside and say the dumbest thing ever.

"Hello?"

chapter sixteen

I'm going to ding myself for that. If someone answered, I'd run out of my skin.

It smells like mildew, old people, and . . . and slavery. I'm shaking and walking as softly as I can. I need to take care of business and get out of here. Now, where's that ledger?

I cover my nose, take a few more steps, but leave the door open in case I need to dash.

What's all this stuff doing in here?

To the right, against a short wall, is a thick wooden table, a child's chair, and two full-size ones. The legs on the child's chair are uneven, and it leans to the right. That must be the chair Grandma told me about. Down the wall from the table is a fireplace made of bricks. And in front of it are two wooden rocking chairs. The fireplace is clean, but as I get closer, I notice a huge pot hanging from inside. Maybe when the electricity goes out at Grandma's house, she comes in here to cook.

On the other side of the room is a wall full of pictures. One day I'll check them out, but not today. I look down on the floor and notice a box of stuff, a wicker basket with folded blankets inside, a black sewing machine, and . . . is that a typewriter?

This shack must be where my family stores junk. So I didn't really lie to Sunny when I told her it wasn't a slave shack. It really *is* a storage shed!

Okay, where's that ledger? My eyes catch a glitter on top of a small wooden stand, so I shuffle over to check it out. It's a huge book with two gold Ls in the center and the word LEDGER engraved at the very top. Booyah!

I'll just take a quick look at Laura Elaine's stuff and get out of here. I pick up the ledger, carefully walk it over to the table, and take a seat in one of the bigger chairs. I'm ready to read whatever's inside. As I open the book, my goose bumps get goose bumps. And I can't decide if I want to stay or run.

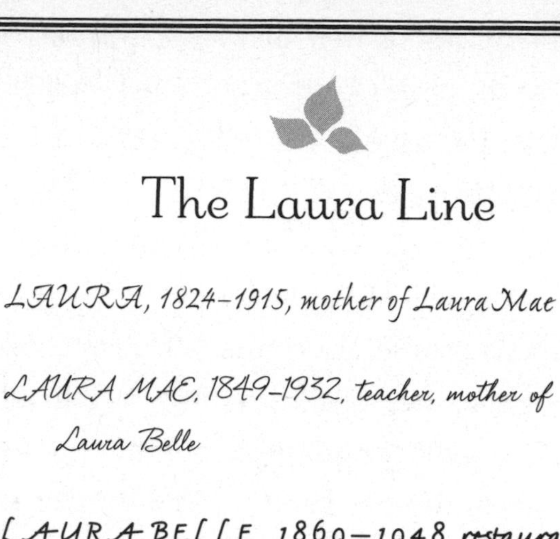

The Laura Line

LAURA, 1824–1915, mother of Laura Mae

LAURA MAE, 1849–1932, teacher, mother of Laura Belle

LAURA BELLE, 1869–1948, restaurant owner, mother of Laura Ann

LAURA ANN, 1900–1958, athlete, mother of Laura Jean

LAURA JEAN, 1924–1995, seamstress and model, mother of Laura Elaine

LAURA ELAINE, 1941–1966, journalist, mother of Laura Lee

LAURA LEE, 1958– , loan officer, mother of Laura Rachel

LAURA RACHEL, 1976– , scientist, mother of Laura Eboni

LAURA EBONI, 2001–

Who put my name in here? I turn the page, looking for answers. Each page is protected in a plastic cover. The first one reads:

LAURA RACHEL

My mother's not dead, so what's her stuff doing in here? I flip the page and find pictures of her in elementary, middle, and high school. There's one of her doing her first science experiment at this table! Here's a letter from Texas State University letting her know she didn't get accepted. And another one from a college in Louisiana. I didn't know Mom had such a hard time getting into college. Well, at least she didn't give up. And her alma mater, Texas Southern University, is a good school. That's where she met Dad, and got her degree in science.

On other pages behind Mom's name, I find certificates, diplomas, her letter of acceptance into the Army Reserve, a pay stub where she wrote on the top, "First paycheck." Besides the pay stub and the college rejection letters, I knew about all that other stuff.

I turn the next page and it reads:

LAURA LEE

There might be some good stuff in here, like an old love letter to Grandpa or something. Or maybe even one to an old boyfriend! Let's see, she's got her marriage certificate on one page and my mom's birth certificate behind it. I turn the next page and find the ticket stub from the baseball game we went to last Sunday. Why would she put *that* in here?

Up in that Laura Line family tree, it said she was a loan officer. What is that? She doesn't have anything in here about it. Is this all she's going to leave in the ledger?

What a bust. If the next one isn't Laura Elaine, I'm out of here. I turn the page, and there she is.

LAURA ELAINE

Okay. Here we go. The first page shows pictures of people I've never seen before. There's a letter from a publishing company, telling her they don't have any openings but thanking her for applying. Here's a letter from March 12, 1959, welcoming her to the *Brooks County Tribune* and mentioning her work hours are eight o'clock in the morning until six in the evening. Plus her salary will be ninety cents an hour, with a raise to one dollar in sixty days after her probation period.

I turn the page and find a newspaper article about a new church, and the byline reads "Laura E. Holmes." Okay. That's kind of cool. The next few pages have more pictures. But it's the last page that floors me. It's a eulogy written by Laura Jean Upshaw.

I go back to the family tree and find out that Laura Jean Upshaw is Laura Elaine's mother. On the front cover of the funeral program is a picture of Laura Elaine. She's so young. I rush back to the Laura Line and subtract the year of her birth from the year of her death. She died at twenty-five? What happened to her? Was she sick? I'm not sure I want to read this, but I know I have to.

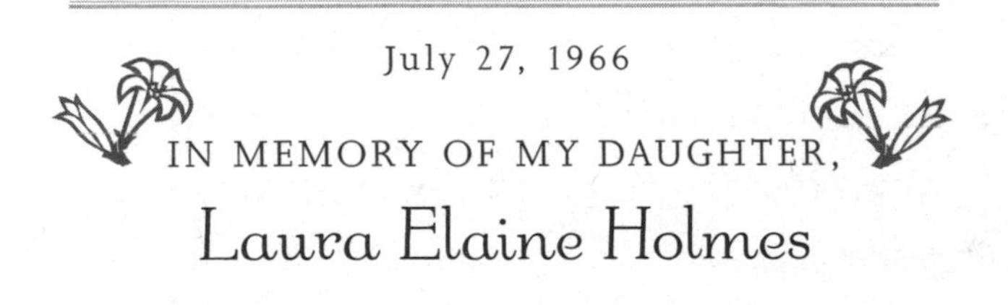

I only had one daughter, so of course I named her Laura. Laura Elaine. She was my youngest child. I loved her so much. When she was small, I could always find her reading to the farm animals while sitting under a tree or pretending to be an actress or a model like me inside the shack on our property.

Even though Laura Elaine loved to read,

she had an even greater passion to write. When she got old enough, she volunteered at the Brooks County Tribune *just so she could be close to the news. The editor loved my Laura Elaine so much—and I'm sure she bugged him plenty—that he gave her a small writing assignment. She did such a good job that he eventually hired her.*

After she got that job, we'd find her in the shack on the farm at all hours of the night, typing away on the typewriter her boss gave her. But last Monday, she went down to Gator Lake. I don't know why. Laura Elaine was an excellent swimmer, but she knew better than to swim alone. I guess I'll never know what happened.

Even though she's gone, she left me her only daughter, Laura Lee, and that beautiful little girl looks just like her mother. I miss my Laura Elaine, but I know all the Lauras in heaven will take care of her.

I close the book and place it back on the stand. I'm done with the ledger for today. Here's the very first Laura that I never met, and not only is she dead, but nobody has a clue about what actually happened. Did she do a report on something that got her in trouble with some bad guys? Did she get murdered? What about an autopsy? Was there an investigation?

This is the kind of stuff I need to keep away from my classmates. They'll ask questions about her, and I don't have the answers. I'll look like an idiot. And that's all I need right now: another nickname. Fat Larda the Idiot.

My stomach knots, and I put my elbow on the table just to hold my head in my hand. I can't let them make fun of her like they make fun of me.

And why would Troy like this story? My nostrils flare with every breath. My body tightens as I reach for the ledger, reopen it, and read the eulogy again. And again. Laura Elaine. Dead at twenty-five and nobody knows what happened.

As I turn to leave, I see the pictures on the wall. One is of a woman sitting at a table, working away on a typewriter.

My eyes slide downward to the floor where the typewriter sits. I look back to the picture. Could it be hers? It has to be. I back away from it and bump into the table. Maybe I better sit back down.

I inhale a big breath of air, remembering something that has not crossed my mind until this very moment.

Laura Elaine's been in here.

And I may be sitting in the exact seat she sat in

when she typed on that busted typewriter.

I dash out of the shack toward my pitching area. Maybe I should throw. But I don't feel like it. I stop and turn toward the house. Wait. I'm not ready to face Grandma and talk about about what I've read or what I've seen. I turn again, and now I'm facing the crosses, the actual Laura Line.

It's still daylight so I'm not afraid. The crosses seem taller and straighter as I look at them from an angle. I've walked by them with Mom before, but I didn't pay attention to any of them.

Now I'm looking for a specific one.

It's a slow walk, like a funeral processional. I'm not sure what's making me move, but I'm moving toward the Line. I'm thinking she's going to be at the far end, but she's not. She's the first cross on this end, closest to the house. I examine everything, from the dirt and big rocks at the base of the cross to the very top. In the center, someone has carved into the wood:

LAURA ELAINE

Why didn't they carve in her last name? As I look down the Line, I notice that none of the Lauras have their last names carved into their crosses, only first and middle. What about their husbands? Weren't they married? What if none of them were married except Grandma and Mom? I rush to the house, and Grandma's in the kitchen, smiling.

"Hey, Baby Girl! I saw you go inside the shack! I've got a chocolate cake in the oven, because this is a day to celebrate!"

I interrupt her. "Why aren't the last names on the crosses? Did Laura Elaine do all her typing in the shack? What happened to her? No, Grandma, I don't want any cake. I read the story about your mom and it was the saddest story ever. Whatever happened to her is no reason to celebrate."

Grandma wipes her hands on her apron. "Neither the ledger *nor* the shack is about death. They're about a line of very strong and powerful women. The Laura Line. Laura is really the only name needed on those crosses, but the middle names were added so we could tell them apart. The Line is a beautiful thing, Baby Girl."

All my sadness stops in the pit of my gut. "My stomach hurts. I just want to cry for Laura Elaine, Grandma. I don't know why you've never told me that story. Why did you wait for me to read it in the ledger?"

I plop down in my chair near the refrigerator as Grandma takes her time putting dinner on the table. She sits, says a prayer, passes me a bowl of steamed carrots, and answers my question.

"Some things were meant to be written. Other things are told from one Laura to another."

I take the carrots. "Like what?"

Grandma stops eating and stares at the ceiling, blinking a lot but smiling, too.

"Like how I'd sneak into the shack at night, dressed in my pajamas. I should've been in bed, but I'd sit in that little uneven chair while Momma worked on her newspaper articles. I'd sing to her, and she kept a coloring book and crayons out there for me. I've got great memories of life with Momma in the shack. That's all I have left of our time together."

I think about that. I've got lots of memories of me and my mom doing tons of stuff at a bunch of different places. Hearing Grandma talk about her one-place memory makes me even sadder. Even though I want to ask if she ever found out what happened to Laura Elaine, this doesn't feel like the right time. I've had enough shack sadness for one day.

I shrug. "Okay. What else makes the shack so special to you?"

I'm thinking I've made my point until Grandma gets up and walks to the kitchen window. I'm sure she's looking at the shack, but then she shocks me.

"I was born in there."

I drop my fork. Grandma's shaking her head.

"Can you believe it? Right in front of the fireplace, the same spot where our first Laura died. And here's another Laura Line connection: The year I was born is the year Laura Ann died of pneumonia. That's what my grandmother, Laura Jean, told me. I guess that's why when I'm in there: I feel special, energized and surrounded by the Laura Line. Did you feel that too?"

"Feel what?" I'm still stunned and overloaded by the info she just gave me.

After a moment, I fire a question at her. "Why isn't your birth certificate in the ledger?"

She turns from the window and takes my hands. "My birth certificate says I was born at home. It doesn't say inside the shack. Some things are better *heard* than read. There's so much I have to tell you. Your mother knows most of the stories, but I still have so many more to tell and I'm going to tell them. As the oldest living Laura, it's my responsibility, and I won't let the history of the Laura Line die."

Grandma raises her chin. Mine elevates, too, and I don't even know why I lifted it. I'm not sure what's happening, but it's happening inside me. Maybe my knower just connected with Grandma's. Right now, I feel closer to her than I ever have.

"I'll try to remember the stuff you tell me. And your mom sounds awesome."

Grandma shakes her head. "She was. But the shack's

getting old and tired. It's wearing down. Things are falling apart inside."

She comes back to the table and picks up her fork, and I watch her eat for a moment. She just dropped some big-time history on me about the shack. I have to admit that some of that stuff was meganews, especially the part about her being born in there.

But just because it's Grandma's birthplace, that doesn't erase all the bad stuff that happened there before she was born. Grandma's story is just one good one against a hundred bad ones. The shack was built for slaves, not newborns.

I wipe my nose as I think about how that place reeks with shame. And if I can smell slavery in there, I'm sure my classmates will, too. Then they'll wonder, just like I do, why we would keep such a horrible thing on our farm. And I can already hear them whispering:

Fat Larda's family can't tell the difference between an heirloom and a slave's room.

My shoulders tighten and my neck hurts. That field trip's got to get canceled.

I push the carrots around the plate as I think about the ledger. I have to admit that book wasn't boring. I don't even know why it's in the shack. So far, none of the Lauras were slaves. I mean, I wouldn't mind putting that book in my backpack and taking it to history class.

Wait . . . there's an idea! Maybe that's the perfect compromise.

I swing my legs under the table and remember something I saw in the ledger that confused me. And only Grandma's going to have the answer.

"Why did you put the baseball ticket stub in the ledger?"

She nods and smiles. "All these years I thought it was just a silly pastime. But after seeing how much you loved it, I wanted to learn more about baseball—and I actually like it. That was a lesson for me. And I've found something else I like to do!"

I give her a big smile. "I'm glad you like baseball, Grandma."

She holds her glass of iced tea toward me. "Here's to learning how to see things differently."

I lift mine to touch hers.

Clink.

We take a sip of our tea and giggle. After dinner, I excuse myself and head to my room. I've got a totally different focus right now, and that's letting Mrs. Jacobs know I've come up with a good replacement for the field trip.

So I turn on my computer and look up the faculty

email addresses for Royal Middle School. There she is: Edna Jacobs, History Teacher. I shoot her an email asking her if we can discuss the field trip tomorrow. Moments later I get a reply:

> Looking forward to it! I'll bring my lunch.
> Let's plan to talk in my classroom. It should
> be empty during your lunchtime.
> Mrs. Jacobs

There's a knock. "Laura Eboni, I've got something for you."

I get up, open the door, and grin. Mmm. Chocolate cake.

Then I get a better idea. "Hey Grandma, will you make me a lunch for tomorrow? It's kind of a special day."

Her whole face smiles. "I'll make you the best lunch ever!"

chapter seventeen

Grandma must have thought I said I was going to feed the hungry. This isn't a sack lunch, it's a meal plan for an entire week. I'm trying to stuff my grocery-sack lunch in the locker when Sage walks up with Sunny and the other Pink Chips. I stare at them.

"What?"

Sage speaks up. "Laura, you're my best friend, right?"

I move from low-key to red alert. "Is that some sort of trick question?"

Sunny moves in front of Sage and takes over the conversation.

"We've invited *your* best friend to be a member of the Pink Chips."

I shrug. "And?"

Sunny continues. "It's time for her initiation."

I shrug again. "So?"

Sunny gives a sly grin. "We've decided to do the initiation in your slave shack."

I show them my hand. "Psh! You must've hit your head this morning, 'cause you're talking crazy."

I scan the area to see if anyone else heard Sunny's ridiculous statement, then turn to face them. Sage has a quirky smile, but it's nothing compared to the smirk on Sunny's face. The other Pink Chips stand behind her and appear carefree and bored. I make myself clear.

"First, it's not *my* slave shack! But it definitely isn't yours for the using, either."

Sage puts her arm around me. "Please, Laura. It won't take a long time."

I squint at Sunny. "That was weak and underhanded."

Sage removes her arm from my shoulder. "Laura, listen to me."

"Back up, Sage. Honestly, this isn't even about you. It's between me and Sunny."

Sunny pouts at Sage. "Awww. What a terrible best friend you have, Sage. Everything's about *her*. Oh, well. That was your chance. It's either the shack or nothing. Leaving."

They walk off. Sage's face is red, and I can tell she's going to blow. So I try to calm her.

"Sage, you don't need the Pink Chips!"

She roars back. "But you do! Think about it, Laura. We're C-listers. But the Pink Chips are A-list girls. I know you're trying to get the field trip squashed, right?"

I nod.

Sage quiets down. "This is your plan B. You gotta have one. Look, you and I both know that if Sunny Rasmussen says the sky is pink, it's pink."

I grab my English and math books from my locker. "For some."

Sage keeps going. "So if she steps inside that shack and likes it, your reputation climbs over the clouds. And the field trip becomes the hottest ticket in town."

I hadn't thought of it that way. "But I hate Sunny!"

"And you hate the shack."

My brain, eyes, and lips freeze. Sage keeps talking.

"It's just a backup plan. Plus what is the absolute worst thing that can happen? Your history class boos you? You get laughed at? Come on, Laura. It's a great plan B."

I chew my bottom lip. "I don't know. I need a minute to think about this."

Sage folds her arms across her chest. "Sunny's right! It's not about what I want; it's about what *you* think. Is that what you're saying?"

I slam my locker closed. "No! Sage, no, that's not what I'm saying."

She faces me. "Then prove it." Her hand rests on my shoulder.

"I will always . . ."

The warmth of her hand is working its way down my shoulder. My arm feels like it weighs five hundred pounds and I can't lift it. Sage sighs and says it again.

"I will always . . ."

I push her hand off my shoulder. "I can't! It doesn't have anything to do with you."

"Yes it does, Laura! And if you cared, you'd help me. I'm always there for you, aren't I? I've always got your back, don't I?"

"Yeah, you do, but . . ."

"And it's not like you care about the shack."

Mist forms on my face, and sitting on the tip of my tongue is a confession that maybe I was wrong about the shack. But I'm not ready to confess anything. So I agree with Sage.

"You're right. I don't care about it at all."

She begins to cry. "Then why won't you help me? It's not like we're going to be in there overnight. Probably an hour, tops. And then I'll be a Pink Chip.

That's all *I* want, Laura."

I'm breaking down. My voice gets whiny. "Sunny's trying to force me to let her see the shack before the field trip on Friday. And she's using you. Again."

Sage wipes tears from her face. "Please, Laura. Just this one thing."

I'm about to say no when Sage hits me where she knows it will hurt.

"It's always just been us, Laura. We've been each other's only friend because of . . . you know. If it were you, I'd never make you beg me for help."

In my mind, I watch the arrow on my Sage's-best-friend meter slip to SELFISH. She's always got my back, no matter what. As if she knows what I'm thinking, she places her hand back on my shoulder.

"I will always . . ."

I lift my arm and place my hand on her shoulder. ". . . have your back."

We flick imaginary dust off, but before Sage gets too excited, I lay down the law.

"Thirty minutes. You tell Sunny she's got half an hour in the shack on . . . Monday?"

Sage hugs me in the hall. "Thank you, Laura! Oh, my gosh! It's going to happen! I need a new outfit and maybe new shoes for my big day. Something to not make me look so . . . you know. You said Monday, right?"

I nod. "Yeah, Monday. I know you don't think I've got your back, but I do."

Sage sniffles. "I knew you'd come through for me. And I've got a feeling this is going to be great for the field trip, too. See you at lunch."

"Oh, right, about lunch. I won't be in the cafeteria today. I've got some important business to take care of, and I'm doing it during my lunch period."

Concern covers her face. "You need my help? Is everything okay?"

I put up a hand. "No, I got this. And once I'm finished with my, uh . . . business meeting, everything should be better than okay."

Sage grins again. "Wow. You sound so grown-up. A business meeting. Cool."

"Whatever, Sage. You're selling newspapers after school, right?"

She nods. "Yep."

"I'll make sure the bus driver waits on you. See you later."

I'm trying to walk away, but Sage stops me.

"Laura Eboni Dyson, thanks to you, this is going to be the best day ever."

She's laughing, walking on the tips of her Sketchers, bouncing down the hall more than anyone her size should ever bounce. But I know at this moment, Sage doesn't care that kids are pointing at her. She hasn't had many bounce-worthy moments, and I'm probably the only person in the hall right now who can relate.

At 11:30, I walk into an empty history classroom. It feels weird being in here so early, but it looks and smells the same. I'm not sure what to do, so I stand near Mrs. Jacobs's desk. The talk with Sage pops into my head. Never in a million years would I have considered Sunny Rasmussen as my plan B. Sage is right about one thing: Whatever Sunny says at Royal is golden.

Soon, the door opens, and Mrs. Jacobs walks in.

"Sorry I'm late, Laura. Had to warm up my lunch. Come sit at my desk. I see you brought your lunch, too. Wow, it looks like you've got a lot to eat! Good!"

I reach into the bag and pull out a note:

I hope you enjoy eating your lunch as much as I enjoyed making it. Love you.

Mrs. Jacobs looks away, but I can tell she read it. I reach back into the bag and pull out a ham and cheese sandwich big enough for a family of six. Mrs. Jacobs's eyes bug out, but then she smiles and opens her thermos. I feel inside the bag again, grab a bowl, and pull it out. It's got a see-through top on it with a plastic fork taped to the top. The bowl's full of fruit. I'll eat that first.

There's more, so I reach inside and pull out two pieces of the chocolate cake from last night. I cut my eyes to Mrs. Jacobs, and again she looks away. My face is warm and I bet she thinks I eat like an oinker. The last thing I find in the bag is long, cold, and wrapped in foil. Mrs. Jacobs giggles.

"That's iced tea. I can tell."

I've actually taken over Mrs. Jacobs's desk with my megalunch. "Sorry about all this food, Mrs. Jacobs. I didn't know—"

She interrupts me. "It's just how Laura Lee shows love. I'm used to it. So, anyway, let's get started on our meeting."

I take the top off the fruit bowl. "Ms. Jacobs, let's talk about the field trip a little more."

"Excellent! I'm all ears."

"I want you to know that I went inside the shack."

Her smile dwindles from her face as she stares into my eyes.

"Good for you, Laura."

I unwrap my party-size sandwich. "There were no shackles, no cotton on the floor, no pictures of the *Amistad*, nothing."

Mrs. Jacobs blows on her soup but keeps watching me. I've got her right where I want her.

"And my grandmother—your BFF—told me the shack's getting old and worn down and she thinks it's going to just fall apart. So I had this idea that maybe Grandma might allow me to bring the ledger to school and—"

She interrupts me. "Absolutely not. That book is priceless. It should never leave the shack." Her head tilts to the side. "How much of the ledger have you read?"

I keep my head down as I eat a piece of melon. "Some of it."

She fires another question. "And what do you know about the pictures on the wall and how they fit in to the whole reason why the shack is such a historical monument?"

I hold up a finger. "The shack's not a historical monument."

Mrs. Jacobs nods. "Not officially yet, but it should be. I keep trying to get your grandma to register that place, because it's full of historical significance."

I drink some tea. "What are you talking about, Mrs. Jacobs? I went into the shack, looked around, came out . . . nothing. No big deal. I wish I could get Grandma to see that."

She goes silent again. I take a bite of my sandwich

and realize I'm almost full. Mrs. Jacobs leans back in her chair. "Maybe you should try to see what your grandma sees! I see it, and I'm sure your classmates will see it, too!"

"What? You're not going to cancel the field trip?" I'm fighting back tears. "But Mrs. Jacobs, I just told you there's nothing in there! It's just an old run-down dirty slave shack. They're going to make fun of me! Please . . . just cancel it."

Her expression turns to concern. "Are you going back into the shack?"

I grimace at the thought. "Doubt it."

She puts the top on her thermos and slides it into her lunch bag. I'm thinking this conversation is a bust until she says something crazy.

"I'm going to offer you a deal, a trade. But you have to agree to honor your end of the deal if you're wrong. I'll agree to honor mine if you're right. Interested?"

A yellow caution flag waves in my head. I lean back and brace myself.

"I'm listening."

She continues. "First, let me be very clear to you. I don't have to do this. I could ignore your request and carry on with my field trip plans. But because your grandma is my . . . BFF, I'm going to tell you that I've already been inside the shack. I've seen everything, several times."

I don't move. Then Mrs. Jacobs says something that loosens me.

"But this isn't about what I think. It's about what *you* think. So you go back inside that shack, and if you can't find one amazing thing—just one—that lines up with what we've been studying over the past few weeks, then I'll cancel the field trip."

I nod. "Deal."

She holds up her hand. "Wait, I'm not finished. But if you go inside the shack and find something that does line up with the history of slavery, and it's so amazing that it makes you proud of the shack and your ancestors, you'll be honest enough to admit it and never talk about canceling the field trip again. Deal?"

I've never negotiated with a teacher before, but I have to take this offer. She holds out her hand. I lean forward and shake it, because to me, this is a no-brainer. But before I let go, I want to make sure we have an understanding.

"So, basically, I have to find something amazing in the shack that relates to slavery and will make me proud of the Laura Line and the shack. If that doesn't happen, you'll ax the trip?"

She nods and leans in toward me. "I'll ax the trip."

"Fine." I exhale, let go of her hand, and put all of my lunch leftovers, except for my drink, back in the grocery bag. Then I relax, sip on my quart of iced tea, and feel in control of the whole situation.

I even smile, because to me, that field trip is as good as canceled.

chapter eighteen

This gravel road is the only thing standing between me and my mission. I've got a military rhythm in my walk as I take the same route to the shack that I took on Wednesday, but this time, I'm not going in there for Troy. I'm excited and embarrassed and ashamed and curious, all at the same time. My emotional drama needs to step aside, because I've got a bet to win.

I've gotta shake these jitters. I know the bet is going to be won or lost in the ledger, so as soon as I walk inside, I place my backpack on the table and go get it. Once I open the book, I run my finger down the Laura Line family tree. I've read the ones for Mom, Laura Rachel; Grandma, Laura Lee; and Grandma's mom, Laura Elaine. The next Laura is Laura Jean.

There she is.

Laura Jean

There's a picture of a little girl sewing at a table. She's awfully young to be sewing. Is that Laura Jean? She can't be older than eight. I turn the next page. It's a picture of a formal gown. I run my finger across the picture, imagining what the dress feels like. Did Laura Jean make this?

I sit up and clear my throat. Maybe she did make it. And even though it may be kind of cool, it's not *amazing.* Kids do stuff like this all the time. And I don't think sewing is that hard. I've sewn before. I made a handkerchief for Dad one year for Father's Day. Sewing must run in the family, and the only thing Laura Jean's story does is give me a clue to where it all began for us.

It still doesn't have anything to do with slavery. Though I have to give her props for this bangin' dress. It's gorgeous.

I can't believe the fancy lace and pearls around the hem and the neckline. Even though it's old, I could wear that on my wedding day and I wouldn't be mad. It doesn't take long for the daydream to take me down the aisle with Dad beside me. Troy's standing at the front with Shane and the minister. I'm wearing the dress Laura Jean made, and the pearls are all shiny and the lace is so . . .

I startle myself out of that special edition of Troy TV. What the what am I doing? I need to focus, because I've got to get this field trip canceled!

I turn the page and find a letter to Laura Jean, congratulating her on a successful production despite all the things that went wrong. Was Laura Jean a movie producer? Here's another letter apologizing that the fabric she ordered was not going to be delivered in time for her production.

I'm almost through with Laura Jean's pages when I turn to the last one and my eyes switch to high beam. I exhale without inhaling first as the words on the fashion show program seem to leap out at me. It reads FASHION EXTRAVAGANZA at the top. Is this the production the other letters were talking about? It has to be! In the center of the program is a woman, smiling, both hands raised in the air. In capital letters above her head it reads:

INTRODUCING LAURA JEAN UPSHAW,
MODEL AND FASHION DESIGNER

Uh-oh, maybe I just found *amazing*. I take a long look at the picture. Is that really her? It can't be. I scoot away from the table and walk to the wall of pictures. I scan the one with the woman in a simple, church-ready dress. Her lips are shiny, so I bet she's wearing lipstick. That's got to be her, next to the sewing machine, showing off her work. I wonder if she made her own outfits for her shows, especially since she was a seamstress.

Wait a minute.

My eyes lower to the floor, next to the typewriter, then back at the picture. The sewing machine in the picture and the one on the floor are identical. The one on the floor has the word SINGER in white letters on the top of it. So does the one in the picture. I walk over to the one on the floor, lean over, and touch it.

Sweet Sister of Sewing Sensations! It's Laura Jean's, I just know it. I bet she used that sewing machine to make all the dresses she modeled. How cool is that! I can just imagine how awesome she must have felt modeling a dress she made herself. I start to sashay around the room, but then I stop. Laura Eboni Dyson, snap out of it! Get your mind on the reason you came in here!

But another thought causes me to flinch as if someone has stuck me with a sewing needle. I'm zoned in on her picture, push-pinned to the wall.

The chills come back. Without taking my eyes off her picture, I slowly walk backward as my heart thumps a hard beat I'm not used to feeling. I've been so impressed with her sewing that I didn't pay much attention to Laura Jean. And now she's all I see because, as Mom would put it, Laura Jean is a full-figured woman.

And a model.

And a fashion designer.

I can't believe how long her lashes are and how gorgeous they look on those wide round eyes. Her short hair is parted on the right side and combed over, but even in this black-and-white picture, I can see the perfect tiny wave patterns in her hairstyle. I should have had her picture taped to my English report on why I want to be a professional model. That would have shut everybody up!

I get my swerve on and sashay around the shack just like Laura Jean must have done back in the day. I pooch my lips and tilt my head just enough to look sophisticated but not snobby and prance around like I'm all that. Every once in a while, I check out her picture just to be sure I'm looking the part.

Suddenly, my swerve is stuck and the desire to pretend I'm a model disappears. As I inch closer to the picture of Laura Jean and her sewing machine, my excitement is replaced with dizziness and confusion. I was so caught up in her being thick like me that I didn't notice all the stuff in the background.

Laura Jean's picture shows a fireplace with a cooking kettle inside the hearth that looks identical to the one that's behind me. Also in the photo, the ledger's on the same stand, in the same spot it is right now. My goose bumps come back when I study the table and two chairs in that picture and glance over my shoulder at where I've been sitting. No way.

But where's Grandma's little chair? Oh, that's right! Grandma's dad, who made the little chair, wasn't born yet! This picture rocks!

Laura Jean sewed in here. And I bet she sashayed around this room like I'm doing, maybe dreaming of the day she'd become a fashion designer and a model. All her attempts and failures went into the ledger. Maybe she used them to make her more determined. And then when she hit it big, she put that copy of her program in the ledger, too.

I sit back in the chair and run my fingers across the plastic holding Laura Jean's program and realize I just learned two awesome things:

1. Laura Jean was not a slave, and what she did had nothing to do with slavery.
2. Modeling is in the Laura Line. And now I know where I got the desire.

Even though Laura Jean's story is the closest I've come to *amazing*, it still has nothing to do with slavery or what we've studied in history class. It's cool to learn about her, but it's time to move on.

I look out the window and realize it's still early. Maybe I'll look at one more Laura and then leave. Before I move on, I take another look at Laura Jean's program cover.

I'm kind of proud of her.

Okay, who's next? I turn to the next cover page.

LAURA ANN

There's a birth certificate dated 1924 on the first page. It belongs to Laura Jean, Laura Ann's daughter. I guess Laura Ann was proud of her baby girl! I examine it closely and find out Laura Jean was born right here in Brooks County. Okay, that's pretty cool. The next page holds Laura Ann's marriage license from 1922. Wow, this stuff is ancient.

The rest of her section is thick—and the pages are heavy. I flip the cover sheet and find a piece of cardboard with three blue ribbons and a gold medal on it inside a plastic sheet. I take a closer look at the awards. They're for track and field. One is for hurdles, one for a relay race, and one for a javelin throw. I can't tell what she got the gold medal for.

I didn't know there were athletes in the Laura Line. Mom runs like she's on fire from any kind of ball thrown her way, and she flips past the ESPN channels as if they're not in service. And I've never heard Grandma talk about any sports until she got this major crush on baseball. I turn the page, and there's another piece of cardboard with more ribbons. Laura Ann must have been awesome!

I can't believe we've got a track and field star in the family. Maybe she's the beginning of the athletic genes in the line, just like Laura Jean is the beginning of the sewing part. I move back from the table and walk to the wall of pictures again. That's got to be her in the shorts and white V-neck sweater, holding a ribbon and that javelin spear, standing near a young tree that's barely taller than she is.

The way those trees are grouped together looks familiar.

Wait a minute.

I rush to the door and poke my head out to study the trees in my pitching area. I knew I recognized it. Laura Ann's standing in my stadium!

My eyes dance back and forth from Laura Jean's picture to Laura Ann's. Laura Ann is thinner, but not by much. I wonder how she was able to run so fast with that extra weight. I wonder if other track runners made fun of her. I guess it doesn't matter.

She did it. And she's got the ribbons to prove it.

I turn the page and find a letter dated July 16, 1921. This is antique old. I bet if I take it out of the cover, it'll just turn to dust and blow away. That's double awesome.

The letter is signed by Laura Ann and it's written to her mother. I go back to the family tree and see that Laura Ann's mother was Laura Belle. All these Lauras are confusing me, but I keep them in order thanks to the family tree. I guess if Laura Ann is writing to her mother, then they didn't live in the same city. This should be good.

July 16, 1921

My Dearest Mother,

Greetings from France. I am well and hope you are, too. Did you get my letter last month? Three weeks ago I tried to qualify to represent France in the very first International Track Meet for Women, taking place in Paris in the next year. Coach Pierre thought my best chance for qualifying would be in the one-hundred-yard dash and the baseball throw. Only the first and second place finishers go on to train and compete at the international games.

In the qualifying rounds, I finished fourth in the one-hundred-yard dash and second in the baseball throw. I qualified in the baseball throw, but Pierre claims my name was added to the roster in error. In private, Pierre apologized, explaining that I have been in France for so long that he forgot I was American, and if the officials found out, the entire French team would be disqualified. I feel like he tricked me.

As you know, keeping the fact that I am an American a secret was part of my deal with Pierre when he signed me to the French team. But now that women's track and field is going international, I may not have a chance to compete with this team anymore. I'm so disappointed.

I really want to come home. It has been six years since I last saw you. I apologize for what happened in your restaurant before I left for France. Pierre's outburst was wrong when he declared your food unfit for humans. He truly believed your food made me fat and that as soon as he changed the foods I was eating, I'd be much thinner, faster, prettier, and happier. Again, he was wrong.

I've quit the French team and I also quit Pierre. I'm coming home, Mother, and I will help rebuild your restaurant business. I don't know how to fix what happened, but I promise I will try. Please forgive me. I love you.

Laura Ann

I can't breathe. I scoot back from the table and stand to force air into my body. All her momma drama is one thing, but this baseball throw is a major news flash. Why am I *just now* finding out about Laura Ann and her baseball throws? I look back through the ledger and find a red ribbon for track and field with BASEBALL THROW embossed at the bottom. I leave the ledger open and walk to the backyard.

Laura Ann's cross is in the center of the Laura Line. It's the same size as the others and her name is carved in the center of the wood just like everybody else's.

LAURA ANN

First, I look around to be sure Grandma's not in the area. Then I whisper at her cross.

"I just read the letter you wrote to your mom, and seriously, you had issues. First, you let some dude—and I don't care that he was your man—disrespect your mother. That's a category-one violation in the family code. And I'm going to ding you for that. But I don't want to talk about your major mistake right now.

I want to talk to you about something . . . private."

I look around again to make sure Grandma's not watching. Then I let it fly.

"Did Pierre ever call you names because you were big? Did he call you fat? Can you see me? Were you mad about being . . . big? Maybe you did what you did because you hated how you looked. Maybe you wanted to be skinny and beautiful for Pierre. Or maybe the other girls on your track team were skinny and you wanted to be thin like them. I don't know. I'm just askin'."

I walk from the first cross to the last one, thinking about how Laura Ann may have felt. But I still haven't gotten to the reason why I'm really standing here.

"Don't you just love how the ball feels in your hand? When I'm feeling down, I can throw baseballs until I feel better. Did you ever do that?

"I'm glad I read about you, Laura Ann. I think you'd be proud of my curveball and my heater. But seriously, you should have clunked Pierre in the head with a fastball."

I go back inside the shack, check the family tree, and realize I'm more than halfway through the Line. I've only got three more Lauras to go. There may be plenty of soap opera drama, and I'll admit that my family's got talent, but there's nothing about slavery in the ledger. I put the book back on the stand, grab my things, and close the door behind me.

When I walk into the house, there's a package of hot dog buns on the table. There's also a bag of tortilla chips, a jar of nacho cheese dip, mustard, catsup, relish, and a pitcher of iced tea.

I stroll into the living room. Grandma's in her chair watching the analysts talk about an upcoming game. She's sporting a new housedress with baseballs and logos from all the Major League Baseball teams on it. The colors are so bright I can barely stand to look at it. But what bothers me more is that last week, if she had seen that dress on a rack, she would've left it there.

"Grandma?"

She turns around and holds out her arms. "Look what I got at the dollar store!"

I force a smile. "I love it, Grandma! There's a lot of baseballs and . . . colors on that dress."

She points at two logos near her belly. "The Dodgers are playing the Astros today."

Now I can't help but grin. "Sounds like a good game. I'll watch it with you."

She giggles. "Oh, goodie! How was your lunch today? Did you have enough to eat?"

"Plenty."

"I'll make your lunch every day if you want."

I hold up a hand. "Uh, no thanks, Grandma. But it was very good."

She grins and fires another question. "Were you going to practice your pitching tomorrow?"

I'm in shock. "I can if you want me to."

"I need to see a curveball up close. I'll come watch you throw a few. Dinner's on the table. I thought we'd eat ballpark style tonight. Hot dogs are covered up on the stove. Is that okay with you?"

I grin. "It's better than okay, Grandma. It's perfect."

"Well hurry up and make your hot dogs. The game starts in five minutes."

"Okay. I'll make yours, too."

Grandma looks over her shoulder. "I was hoping you'd say that! Mustard only, please!"

I head to the kitchen, thinking about Laura Ann, and I slow my walk to give the situation more thought. To me, even though Laura Ann was a great athlete, she made some major mistakes and she doesn't add up to amazing. I think she was a slave to Pierre, but that doesn't have anything to do with the shack. So as far as I'm concerned, I'm still on track to win that bet.

chapter nineteen

BOOMP . . . BOOMP . . .

I roll over and . . . *KA-BLAM!*

This falling out of bed is getting old.

BOOMP . . . BOOMP . . .

I scramble to my feet and then sit on the edge of my bed.

My heart's thumping as I try to figure out what that noise is and where it's coming from. It can't be the slave zombies coming to get me, because the sun's coming through my window. Is that burned toast I smell?

"Grandma?"

"In the kitchen!"

"Are you okay?"

"No."

I grab my robe at the end of my bed. "Okay, hold on, I'm coming!"

The smell of burned bread is overwhelming. Just as I step out of my room . . .

ZZZZZZZZZZIP! BOOMP . . .

I duck. "Grandma, what was that flying through the kitchen?"

I cover my head and rush to her. There's a bowl of charcoal-black biscuits on the table. She points at them. "I burned those but figured out a way to use 'em."

I scan the kitchen. There's rock-hard biscuits and black crumbs all over the floor.

"Grandma, what are you doing?"

She grabs a burned biscuit, winds up, and hurls it at the trash can against the wall.

ZZZZZZZZZZIP! BOOMP . . .

The biscuit hits the wall and falls into the trash can. I tilt my head at the five black biscuits on the floor, obvious misses, and listen to Grandma explain.

"I've gripped these bad boys different ways and *still* can't figure out how to throw that curveball."

I'm wondering how many people have a grandma who practices curveballs with burned biscuits at 7:30 on a Saturday morning.

She stops and sips her coffee. "I'm ready whenever you are. I can't figure it out."

I giggle. "Oh, that's right. Just give me a second to put on some sweats."

In no time, we're in my pitching area, and I bring the bucket of balls close to the mound.

"Okay, watch carefully. I'll throw a knuckleball, then a curveball."

I explain how the knuckleball doesn't rotate when it's thrown and the strange movement it has on its way to home plate. I show her my knuckleball.

"Batters see it coming, and then right before it reaches them, it drops out of the air like a dead bird. Here, I'll throw another one."

Grandma shakes her head. "No, that's okay. A dead bird pitch sounds sad."

I shrug. "All right, here's the curveball."

I tell her how the ball looks like it's going to miss the plate but then curves back in for a strike.

"Watch."

I throw one and she claps. I grab another ball. "Your turn! Let's see your curveball."

She rubs her hands together. "I'm ready!"

I put the ball in her hand, place her fingers in the right spots, and let her throw a few. Her first one hits the ground before it reaches the glove. She turns to me.

"That wasn't very good, was it?"

I grin. "It was better than the first one I ever threw. Here, try again."

She does, and on her fifth try she hits the side of Dad's glove.

"That was good, Grandma!"

She points her thumb over her shoulder.

"He's outta there!"

I point my thumb over my shoulder, too, and laugh. Grandma hugs me.

"That was so much fun, Laura, but I need to lay this old body down for an hour or so. Now I really do understand why pitchers need rest."

I nod. "I'm going to throw a little more before I come in. Have a good nap!"

I put my earbuds in and turn on the iPod clipped to my pants. My arm's good and warm now. I should be able to make some excellent pitches. I'll throw a few more curveballs.

POP . . . POP.

I grab another ball from the bucket but accidentally drop it. When I reach down to pick it up, I see a pair of brown boots and I almost trip on my pitcher's mound.

I take the earbuds out and smooth my hair. "How long have you been standing there?"

Troy shrugs. "Long enough to see you throw the nastiest curveball ever. Did your dad teach you how to throw? Where did this pitching area come from? It wasn't here last Saturday."

"Dad made it for me on Sunday. You were so busy spraying the garden on Wednesday that you didn't notice. I come out here and throw whenever I want. Why are you here?"

He's still checking out my pitching hookup. "My dad and I cut grass on Saturdays, and I fertilize the garden on Wednesdays. How long did it take you to learn how to throw that curveball?"

"About a week."

Troy looks around, as if he's about to tell me some top-secret information.

"Mine isn't that good. Actually, my curveball . . . doesn't curve."

"Then it's not a curveball. No wonder you guys got the snot beat out of you in the season opener." I give him a baseball. "Let me see how you throw it. Maybe I can show you what you're doing wrong."

He spits, then stands on my mound. "Pitching lessons from a girl? I don't know. I don't have any money to pay you. And I'm not going to do some crazy favor for you, either."

I join him on my mound and get right in his face. "Did I ask you for anything? I'll tell you what. You're here to cut the grass, right? Then go cut it! And get off my mound!"

I put my hands on my hips and wait. But then his shoulders drop as he shakes his head.

"Okay, my bad. That was uh . . . my bad, Dyson. I'll show you my curveball."

He winds up and throws the saddest imitation of a pitch ever thrown.

Plop. Dang.

Grandma's was better. If I were that baseball he just threw, I'd roll somewhere and hide so he could never throw me again.

He looks my way. "See what I mean?"

I'm trying to find nice words to say, but instead, I shift my weight to the other leg.

"Troy, show me how you hold the ball to throw a curve."

He shrugs. "I don't hold it any different than when I throw my fastball."

I frown at him. "Really? And you seriously don't know why the ball won't curve?"

To me, that's just common sense, but then I see his face. It's blank as the pages in a brand-new notebook. So I reach down and take his hand. It's warm, and my breathing speeds up.

But he pulls away. "What are you doing, Dyson?"

At first I'm startled. Then I blast him. "Do you want to learn how to throw a real curveball, or are you happy to get rocked the rest of the season?"

He gives his hand back to me. It's all about concentration, and I need every ounce of mine to keep from screaming with joy. I grab another ball and position his fingers on the laces, then make him do it himself. Once he's holding it right, I show him how to snap off a nasty and unhittable pitch.

"If you don't get that snap in your wrist as you throw, it's not going to work. When you start the windup, and the ball is up here, near your ear, you've got to know what you're going to do with it. Snap that wrist and throw toward the mitt. Give me the ball and I'll show you."

I break off another nasty curveball and Troy grins at me. "That's sick."

I grab another ball from the bucket. "That's not sick. That's strike three. And right after you throw it, stare that batter down with no emotion, like this."

I stand on the mound, appearing unfazed as I stare at home plate. "Got it? No emotion. Look like it's just another day on the mound for you and another strikeout for him. Make the batter feel like you own him, understood?"

Troy's nodding fast. "Yeah, own him. You're right. Let me try. Wow, Dyson! How many guys have you struck out?"

I stare at Dad's glove. "I've never pitched to anyone other than my dad. And sometimes I think he strikes out on purpose."

I back away and watch Troy mimic what I did. His ball starts off straight then suddenly breaks toward Dad's glove.

POP!

Troy freaks. "No way! Did you see that?"

"Yeah! I call that pitch Slimfast. You know, like that diet stuff, because it makes curves. Get it? Go ahead, Troy, throw it again."

He does everything I showed him and looks so good standing there. He throws the pitch again, and this time it lands right inside Dad's glove. Troy bangs his fist into his open hand.

"I can't believe it! That pitch is money!"

A strong voice with lots of bass makes me jump. "Troy! Why aren't you working?"

Troy's freaking out. "Dad, come here a minute!"

A thin man in faded jeans, work boots, a long-sleeved flannel shirt, and gardening gloves comes from the side of the shack. He waves as Troy does the introductions.

"This is Fa . . . uh . . . Laura Dyson. She's Mrs. Anderson's granddaughter."

Mr. Bailey winks. "Nice to meet you. Your grand-mother is a wonderful lady."

Troy grabs a ball from the bucket. "Hey, Dad, watch this."

He grips the ball, goes into motion, and throws a perfect curveball. Mr. Bailey claps.

"That was incredible! Who taught you how to throw that?"

Troy nods my way. Mr. Bailey chuckles. "Where did you learn how to pitch like that?"

"My dad taught me. He was a catcher in college. A really good one."

Mr. Bailey smiles. "I'd have to agree. I'd love to talk baseball with your dad." He turns to Troy. "Next time you pitch, that curveball should be your secret weapon."

Troy chuckles. "Yeah. My secret weapon."

Mr. Bailey pats Troy on the shoulder. "Okay, Slugger, back to work."

Troy watches his dad leave, then turns to me.

"You got a fastball?"

"Uh-huh."

"I bet I could smack it to Jupiter. I've got a bat in the back of Dad's truck. I'll be back."

Troy's gone for only a moment and returns with his bat. He stands in front of home plate.

"Throw your fastest pitch, Dyson. But say good-bye to that ball, because it's history."

Sweet Father of Fiery Fastballs! I can't believe this

is happening! He's got the bat high over his shoulder, waiting for the pitch. I wind up and throw a laser.

SWOOOSH!

He stands there with the bat still high above his shoulder. The ball drops out of Dad's glove and falls behind him. Troy shakes his head as he walks to the mound.

"Trust me, Dyson. Your dad's not striking out on purpose."

I grin and kick at my mound. "I should have let you take a few warm-up swings."

He spits in the dirt. "I don't think that would've helped. Thanks for teaching me that curveball. That was mega. Seriously, you don't know what you did by helping me with that."

"Yes I do. Everybody knows the Pink Chips put you on Blue Chip probation."

He stares at me as if he didn't know. But then, after looking closer into his face, I realize that's not what his eyes say at all. I put my hands on my hips.

"Don't you even care about being on probation?"

He starts grabbing at weeds around the trees. "I've never cared about that Blue Chip stuff. I don't want to be one. They didn't even ask me."

That's a piece of news Sage doesn't know. "So if you don't care about them, then why are you trying to get that curveball right?"

He tenses up again. There's anger in his face, and I'm wondering if this boy's got a demon. "Why are you all in my business, Dyson?"

I turn away from him, put my earbuds back in, and gather the baseballs from around the tree. Right now, it doesn't matter that he's the cutest boy in the world, especially when he talks so mean to me. Maybe he doesn't care about Blue Chips, but after that remark, I'd fill his dimples with cow chips if I had 'em.

I'll never have a need for that kind of attitude. I've got enough drama. And now that I am one hundred percent sure that Troy's a jerk, why am I . . .

There's a tap on my shoulder. I turn around, take the earbuds out, and let him talk.

"That didn't come out right. Can you just give me a break?"

I move to put the earbuds back in, and he caves.

"All right! I'll tell you if you promise to keep it a secret."

By the look on his face, I can tell something's trying to make its way to his throat but it's stuck. Even his dimples are sagging. So I give him all of my attention and soften my voice.

"Seriously, I won't tell anybody. I promise."

"I'm doing it for my dad. Since he lost his company, he doesn't smile much anymore, except when he's watching me play sports. When I play really well, he smiles and seems so happy. But when I don't do good, he still smiles, but I know that smile is fake. I think when my game ain't on, it reminds him that he didn't do good enough to keep his company."

I interrupt him. "Troy, that can't be true."

He frowns again. "How do you know, Dyson? On opening day, I stank up the place. I was a loser, so I reminded Dad that he's a loser. Don't you see?"

I let him know I understand, then grab another ball. "You hang out with your dad a lot?"

Troy pulls a trash bag from his back pocket. "Yeah. Since he made me a partner in his business, we hang out all the time. We do just about everything together. Drives my mom crazy!"

He opens the trash bag, picks up a few twigs, and chuckles. I smile to hide that I feel sorry for him. "That's nice. But what are you going to do when he finds a different job?"

He spits in the grass again. "On the real . . . I hope he never finds one. I know he needs steady work, but I like hanging with him, learning stuff. And you know, we've got a business now."

I nod. "And it's a good business."

Troy agrees. "We just need more customers, that's all. I've got to go, Dyson. Thanks for the curveball lesson. Your fastball is wicked too! You got any more awesome pitches?"

"All my pitches are pure gold! I even named them. I call my curveball Slimfast and I already told you why. My changeup is called Almond Joy because it's my favorite pitch and Almond Joy is my favorite candy. I named my fastball Expresso because it's got lots of mojo behind it. And my knuckleball is called Chuckle Knuckles. Doesn't that sound like an ice-cream flavor at Baskin-Robbins? Uh, can I have two scoops of Chuckle Knuckles?"

I'm in my own world, enjoying the names I picked for my pitches. But when I look at Troy's face, he's just staring at me. I pick up a ball from the bucket.

"Maybe next time you're over here, I'll hook you up with the Chuckle Knuckles pitch."

I'm talking too much, but I can't help it. I'm with the cutest boy in the world, in the woods, talking about one of my most favorite things.

I'm expecting him to say something about my pitches, but instead, he just nods.

"Later, Dyson."

As he walks away, I call to him. "Oh, I almost forgot one megathing."

He turns around, so I grin and point at the shack. "I'm not the first Laura to throw fire."

His eyebrows rise, and I toss a ball up in the air and catch it in my glove.

"That's right. There's a woman named Laura Ann

in my Line. She threw heaters long before I did. Chew on that!"

Troy grins. "No wonder you're so good at pitching! It's in your blood! See you later."

Soon a lawn mower revs up and he's driving around the farm cutting grass. Troy hasn't called me Fat Larda in three whole days. Now he calls me Dyson. I like that! Finally he doesn't see me as fat. He just sees me as someone who can teach him how to throw a curveball.

And I can thank Laura Ann for that.

chapter twenty

After a shower, I can't wait to get dressed and head back into the shack. I don't know what's happened to me and why I suddenly don't mind that ugly place, but I'll have to figure it out later.

Inside the shack, I grab the ledger, then look around a bit, especially at the pictures on the wall. I'm careful not to trip over Laura Jean's sewing machine or Laura Elaine's typewriter. On my way to the table, I put my hand on that little uneven chair, knowing that back in the day, Grandma sat in it and sang and colored in a book as she watched her mother type. That chair is so wobbly! And it's short!

But none of the big chairs have a big-time story like this little one.

I get the ledger and take a seat at the end of the table. After looking at the Laura Line family tree, I see the next Laura should be Laura Belle, Laura Ann's mom. I get to her cover.

LAURA BELLE

Up front is a picture of a building with a sign out front that reads LAURA BELLE'S RESTAURANT. I already knew from Laura Ann's letter that she owned one. So I'm not surprised. I turn the page.

Here's a recipe for pork chops and gravy using lots of different spices. My mouth waters as I check out other recipes for breads, desserts, salads, soups, and stuff.

It seems as if I've been turning pages forever before I get to a newspaper clipping.

LOCAL NEWS

May 4, 1915

A GREAT PLACE TO EAT

Laura Belle's Restaurant, located in Harlem, opened for business one year ago today. With Sunday dinner and daily specials, she's become a favorite around the New York area.

Besides many of the faithful locals, Laura Belle's customers include politicians, famous singers, and musicians.

Laura Belle made the newspaper! Her restaurant must have been the bomb! I turn the page and instead of another newspaper clipping, I find a letter from Laura Belle to her mother, Laura Mae.

September 3, 1915

Dearest Mother,

I pray this letter finds you healthy and surrounded by young students eager to learn! I have included with my letter a newspaper clipping about my restaurant. It is a very nice article and I'd like you to have it. I have not received a letter from you in some time, so I hope to hear from you soon, for I am not doing well.

As you know, since my husband, Charles, died five years ago, I've dreamed of owning a restaurant. Charles loved my cooking and tried to convince me that I could make money selling my meals. Even though I experienced many setbacks and am now in my forties, I made our dream come true and opened Laura Belle's Restaurant.

But last month, I had a terrible incident happen in front of my customers. My Baby Girl, Laura Ann, visited the restaurant with a handsome young man named Pierre. He's a track coach from France, and Laura Ann said he was her boyfriend. As you know, Laura Ann is only fifteen, and even though I clearly did not approve of him, I invited Pierre to eat at the center table in my restaurant.

He ate just a few bites before standing and declaring my food unfit for human consumption. Pierre shouted without stopping, and many of my customers left, some without paying. Pierre even accused my food of being the reason why Laura Ann is overweight and unfit to run track.

Laura Ann and Pierre left the restaurant, and I have not seen them since.

Now, with a heavy heart, I am working long hours to rebuild my customers' confidence in my menu. Some of my regular customers are slowly returning, but I don't know if I can hold on to my restaurant until things return to the way they were.

I heard that my Laura Ann is somewhere in France running track on Pierre's team. I *miss her so much and want her back home. But most of all, Mother, I want you to know that I am not a quitter. I will fight for my restaurant until the end. I don't need anything from you but your love and your prayers.*

I hope to hear from you soon.

Laura Belle

Before I read Laura Belle's letter, Laura Ann was my favorite. But now I'm furious with her again for allowing that French fry named Pierre to make Laura Belle feel so bad. I'm sure the arrow on Pierre's personality meter is stuck on JERK. I close the ledger and refuse to read any more. Instead I pace the floor, trying to think of why Laura Ann would pick a guy like him.

I put on the brakes in the middle of the floor. What am I doing? I've got to finish what I started. There's nothing I can do for Laura Ann except never be like her.

I've only got two more Lauras to go and I'll be finished. And so far, there's nothing to prove Mrs. Jacobs's point. Laura Belle is definitely amazing, but she didn't serve slaves in that restaurant. She didn't cook for slaves in the shack either.

If I'm going to win, I need to get back to the ledger.

But I'm going to give Laura Belle the Mother of the Century award. She deserves it. The next cover sheet says:

LAURA MAE

Her first page holds her marriage license. The next page shows a deed to property in Brooks County, Texas. Is that the deed for this property? Was Laura Mae the first Laura to live here? Does this shack belong to her? I turn the next page to find worksheets for math and spelling exercises. Just by the looks of them, they must be for kindergartners or first graders. The family tree says she was a teacher, so that makes sense.

I race to see how fast I can do the worksheets in my head, but soon, I'm so bored that I'm feeling sleepy. So I flip pages until the worksheets are gone. There's a letter from Laura Mae to her daughter, Laura Belle. Maybe it's the answer she needs to deal with Laura Ann.

October 4, 1915

Laura Belle,

I pray to Almighty God this letter finds you healthy and in good spirits. I got your letter today and read it over and over again. The reason your letter took so long to reach me is because I have moved. Today when I received a small bag of mail from my old mailbox in Philadelphia, your letter was in it.

I'm so sorry about the trouble you had with Laura Ann and Pierre. Don't worry, my Baby Girl. Laura Ann will come to her senses and return home. Your customers will return, too. I will continue to pray for you. I wish I was there to help, and you must know that if you ask me, I will come.

And I'm sure some of the treatment you're receiving is pure jealousy from the wonderful article in the newspaper, recommending folks of all colors eat at Laura Belle's Restaurant!

Since my last letter to you, I have married and moved back to Texas. Now my official name is Laura Mae Richard. My husband is a kind man. He owns a very successful clothing store. I have retired from full-time teaching, but I'll continue to work with a few children just because I love it.

Even though most news is good, it is with great sadness that I write this letter. A note from Mother's closest friend reached me that Mother passed away. She was found in her favorite rocking chair near the fireplace. That is why I returned to Texas, to the place from which I escaped slavery over fifty years ago. We purchased the house where Mother spent her last hours. My husband also bought several acres around it, so we're building a home. I'd like to start a garden underneath these huge oak trees.

I have purchased a ledger to hold on to those things precious to the women in our family. I'll call it the Laura ledger. Please send me what you'd like kept inside the ledger for Lauras in the future and others to remember about you.

I would love some of your recipes, and please send me some of Laura Ann's winning ribbons! I plan to add educational things, for that is what I hope to leave as my legacy.

Laura Belle, we must keep Mother alive in our minds by never forgetting the stories of her youth in Sierra Leone, and of her capture and voyage on the Amistad, where she was chained and beaten until she, along with others, fought and took over the ship. And we must tell of her sacrifice for the four young children held captive on the Amistad, destined for slavery until Mother fought for them, too, and was taken in their place at the innocent age of fifteen.

I am also free because of Mother. When I was thirteen, she entertained the plantation owner and his guests for hours with her beautiful singing as I escaped. I never saw Mother again to thank her in person. And now she is gone. But I am grateful to her friend for making sure Mother got my letters *and that I received the news of her death.*

You've heard Mother's stories many times. You must tell them to Laura Ann, and she must tell them to her children. Do not let Mother and what she did fade in our minds. It is because of her that we exist. And it is because of her that we exist in freedom.

I have made a burial place for her behind her home.

Maybe you will come to Brooks County, Texas. I would like that.

Love, Mother

No . . . No!

I back so far away from the table that I hit the wall of pictures. My head's throbbing, and at any moment I know my legs are going to give out. I rush back to the table, convinced that I missed or added something.

So I read it again. The second time is no better than the first. I quickly turn to the cover sheet for the last Laura.

LAURA

I turn the page, but there's nothing behind it but extra cover sheets and page protectors.

I close the book and wipe my hands down the sides of my pants just in case I got any *Amistad* dust on them. Mrs. Jacobs knew. She knew all along! No wonder she made that bet!

I pace the floor and try to make it all go away in my mind.

That was NOT amazing. That was NOT amazing. It didn't happen. I don't think it could've happened. Not to this Laura. Not the one from the Laura Line. It has to be a lie!

I probably got it all mixed up. Did it say Laura Mae's mother was on the *Amistad*? I run my finger down the letter. There it is. Fifteen years old.

But my eyes seem to make the letters a thousand times bigger than they are as I read the part about her fighting for the four children aboard the *Amistad.* It can't be *those* four. Not the ones we've been reading about in class. She saved them? She's a hero? I rush back to the wall of pictures and look for her. She's not there. I examine every picture, hoping there's some unexplained woman I hadn't noticed before, but there's not.

I back away from the wall, and that's when I see it.

The pictures of the other Lauras line up to form a perfect silhouette. It's a head and forehead that winds inward to make an eye socket and then back out to form a nose. Smaller photos round her lips. I can't move. I remember the three-page *Amistad* handout Mrs. Jacobs gave us. There's no doubt in my mind what I'm looking at. The more I back up, the clearer she becomes.

Sweet Mother of the Laura Line.

It's her.

chapter twenty-one

I rush out of the shack without putting the ledger back on the stand. I run all the way back to Grandma's house. I pass her in the kitchen on my way to my room.

"Baby Girl?"

"Not now, Grandma. I just . . . I can't talk right now."

I close my door and fall across my bed. But the physical proof of it all is eating at me, and I just have to find the facts. Why wasn't the first Laura mentioned on the sheets Mrs. Jacobs handed out?

I rush to my backpack and grab the three-page

handout from last Monday. I scan the names of every one of the captives on the *Amistad.*

No one named Laura.

I go to the computer and Google everything about the *Amistad.*

No one named Laura.

I even play with the names of the other captives on the *Amistad* to see if Laura's name was maybe spelled differently. But it's not.

Wait a minute.

I hold the handout closer to my face and study every detail. Suddenly, I realize something I hadn't picked up on until now. Other than the three little girls—Margru, Teme, and Kagne—there are no females listed on the ship.

I don't remember falling asleep, but I tossed and turned all night unable to get the first Laura out of my mind. The warmth of the sun slicing through my curtains and kissing my face is a welcome feeling.

Knock, knock.

I sit up, wipe the sleep from my face, and realize I'm still in the same clothes from yesterday.

"Come in."

Grandma pokes her head inside.

"I tried to wake you earlier, but you were sleeping so hard that I covered you up and let you sleep. I'm heading to church in thirty minutes. I'll wait for you if you want. Come eat breakfast with me."

"Okay."

I drag my butt out of bed and stare in the mirror at dried lines of tears stretching from the corners of my eyes to the sides of my head. I've been crying in my sleep, and the emotion of it all is still on me. I'm not sure what to do, but I need to do something.

Breakfast smells float under my door and into my nose, so I put on my robe and shuffle to the kitchen. Grandma makes me a plate with eggs, sausages, and fruit. I pour myself a glass of orange juice and take a seat.

"I'm not going to church with you this morning, Grandma."

She sits down at the table. "Is everything okay? Do you need my help?"

I stare at my orange juice. "I'm good."

She picks up her coffee and blows on it. "I understand. I'll be home right after church."

As soon as Grandma's gone, I get dressed and head for the shack. When I open the door, it feels cold inside, colder than I remember. I wonder if I've made it that way with my attitude.

The ledger's still on the table where I left it yesterday when I rushed out so quickly. I sit and stare at it, thinking about all the terrible things I've said about the shack, the Laura Line, and the crosses.

Then I read about all of them, from Mom to the first Laura ever. I can't get that first Laura out of my mind. And I know one thing beyond any doubt.

She's the *amazing* Mrs. Jacobs was talking about.

I read over Laura Mae's letter again and get an idea of the first Laura's personality. She didn't care about having her name in the books. She wasn't looking for compliments about how good a person she was. The first Laura in our line showed us how important it is to help people; not just your family, but everybody. Some may say it wasn't very smart of her to exchange her freedom for a life of slavery. But I get it.

And I'm so proud to be a part of *her* line.

I examine all the pictures on the wall. I rub my hand across the sewing machine and the typewriter. They're real. The women in the Laura Line were kind and smart, and they took chances and wanted to do stuff with their lives. They had boyfriends and husbands and careers. And it all started right here, in this shack. The first Laura lived here and died in here. Every Laura after her has been inside this place, making plans for her future.

I touch the brick around the fireplace, wondering which Lauras touched that same brick before me. My hand slides from the fireplace to my side as I realize how wrong I've been.

Mom was right. I've judged this shack the same way people judge Sage and me. All they can see is the outside, and they have no idea how incredible we really are on the inside. People like Troy never gave me the time of day until he saw me here. Just knowing that I was a Laura seemed to change his attitude.

And here I am, currently the last Laura, denying everything for a reason I can't even remember. I walk out, close the door, and head to the backyard.

I've ignored these crosses many times, and I feel unworthy to even be standing in the grass near them. But there's just something I need to do. I sit down in the grass in front of them and twist one of my braids.

"Hey. This feels weird, but I'm Laura Eboni." I point at the first Laura's cross. "You're the first one, and right now I'm the last, but I don't have any wood with my name on it yet. I don't know if I will ever be as brave as you were. But, anyway, I just wanted to introduce myself since I read about you in the ledger. Grandma, uh, that's Laura Lee, told me some things were meant to be told, not written. I hope she's got something to tell me about you, because I'd really like to know you better."

I think about what she did, and I have to say

something. "I know you saved four little kids from being taken into slavery, and because you did that, they got to go back home. I'm glad you were the first Laura in our line."

I look toward the next cross. "Laura Mae, you're like glue for this group. I mean, you held us together, even after your mother died. And then you made sure Lauras like me would get to know Lauras like you. Thank you, Laura Mae."

I move on. "Laura Belle, you've taught me that I can do and be anything. You had a restaurant, but I didn't think African Americans had any businesses of their own at that time, and on top of that, being a woman restaurant owner is like icing."

I giggle staring at Laura Ann's cross. "You're like the sister I never had, because we're so much alike. I'm athletic, too, but can't seem to find a place around here to show what I can do. The guy I like may or may not be a jerk. But it looks like you figured everything out and did okay. I hope I do okay, too."

I stare a long time at Laura Jean's cross before speaking to her.

"I had no idea where my urge to model came from. Mom never mentioned it. Neither did Grandma. I thought it just popped out of nowhere. I've always wanted to work the catwalk, but when my classmates laughed at me, I almost trashed the thought. Until I read about you in the ledger. Someday I'm going to strut that runway in a bangin' outfit. Thanks, Laura Jean, for showing me that I can."

I'm now at the end of the Line and Laura Elaine's cross.

"I know why Grandma wishes we had met. My best friend works for a newspaper. You'd have liked her, too. Even though you're not here, I know you're with the other Lauras now. I'm sure they are taking good care of you."

I move to get up, but remember one more thing. So I say it.

"And your daughter turned out awesome."

I bow my head and close my eyes for a moment, trying to picture Laura Elaine at the table, typing away on her typewriter without the letter G. I wonder what she did to make up for that. Maybe she had a beautiful handwriting and she could just write one when she needed it.

I guess it doesn't matter. She knew what she wanted and wouldn't let anything stop her from getting it. Now that I think about it, every Laura was like that. It didn't matter what people said or did to discourage them. It didn't matter how cruel life seemed to be. They kept their dreams moving and never let anyone stop them.

Maybe that's the message in the Laura Line.

I think about all the mean things my classmates say to me. I've hated school just because of how I've been treated. Now that I've read the stories in the ledger, I realize that the Lauras before me have already experienced what I'm experiencing now. And they still did great things.

Payback for the Line would be to open up the shack door and let my classmates know what amazing smells like. Then they'd understand that because I'm a member of this elite group, I've got a date with success.

Wait . . .

The tears come automatically as my knower alerts me that I've figured it out. I cover my mouth to stop the loudest cry ever. I thought the first Laura was the amazing thing Mrs. Jacobs warned me about.

She's not.

I'm still going to lose the bet. But I must be the happiest loser in the universe.

I'm ready to get up now. I've done what I needed to do, so when Grandma comes home from church, I'll ask her questions about the Line. I've been inside the shack and around the crosses all morning. It feels different than before, and all I want is more information. I'm sure Grandma has the info I need.

We're at the table, eating sandwiches for lunch, when I ask the question that's been on my mind.

"Did you ever find out what happened to Laura Elaine? I mean, how did your mom drown?"

She puts her sandwich down. "I've been waiting for you to ask me. Yes, we did find out. My grandmother, Laura Jean, demanded an autopsy be done to rule out foul play, especially since she never liked my dad. See, Momma got married and had me at a very young age, and Laura Jean never thought Daddy was good enough for Momma. I loved my daddy. He made that little uneven chair out in the shack. It's the only thing he ever made for me."

I take a bite of my sandwich and zone in on Grandma. "So what happened?"

"The autopsy was done and they couldn't find anything unusual except for a lot of water in her lungs. Then one day, Daddy told us what really happened."

My eyes widen and I stop chewing. "Did he do something to her?"

Grandma shakes her head. "No, but I think it took him a while to realize he couldn't have saved her. I think Daddy needed to know that for sure before he could talk about it."

I put my sandwich down and give Grandma all of my attention.

"Daddy told us on that Thursday afternoon, Momma had surprised him with a basketful of goodies for his lunch and invited him to Gator Lake for a picnic."

I put up a hand. "Wait a minute, Grandma. That's not what the eulogy said. I remember something about her swimming alone."

Grandma's eyebrows rise. "That's what we all thought until Daddy told us what really happened."

I scoot up closer to the table as Grandma continues.

"Gator Lake was their favorite place, and it wasn't too far from Daddy's job at the gas station. According to Daddy, they went, ate, and had a wonderful time. Momma loved to swim, and she decided to take a dip. Daddy chose to eat another sandwich, watched Momma swim, and told her how great a swimmer she was. He said she played jokes on him by going under the water and staying a long time before coming back up. He asked her to stop because it scared him. She just laughed."

I interrupt. "That would probably scare me, too."

Grandma nods. "As she was swimming so beautifully across the lake, she grabbed at her right thigh and completely stopped kicking in the water. Daddy thought she was playing around and laughed at her. He even told her he had to get back to work, so she needed to get out of the water. She didn't answer him. Instead, she went under and didn't come back up."

I put my hand over my mouth. "Grandma . . ."

She closes her eyes. "I know, Baby Girl, but you need to know. Daddy waited, thinking she was playing again, but after a time he rushed into the lake, found her body, and pulled her out. He didn't know CPR, and back then, there weren't any cell phones. So he had to run back to the gas station for help. But it was too late."

That's nothing like I imagined. And I'm feeling bad about asking, because now I've lost my appetite, my heart hurts, and my eyes are tearing faster than I can wipe them.

"I'm sorry, Grandma."

"I am, too. I couldn't have been any older than eight or nine. Even though your great-great-grandma didn't like my daddy, after he told her what really happened, she tried to help him deal with his grief. But he just couldn't stand staying around. He said I looked just like Momma, and he missed her horribly. Eventually he moved away. I got letters and birthday cards from him from all over the country. He never settled down for any period of time. He died seven years ago next month."

I take a long drink of iced tea. "I feel so bad for everybody, especially your dad."

Grandma agrees. "That's why the memories are so important to me."

Eventually my appetite comes back. Grandma and I sit quietly for a long while, eating our lunch, but the silence is too loud.

"Grandma, do you know what you're going to write in the ledger? I mean, you were a loan officer at a bank, right?"

"For a year or two."

"Did you like it?"

"Hated it."

I've got a mouth full of turkey sandwich. "Did you get fired?"

"Nope. Actually they begged me to stay."

Silence.

I'm not sure if I should ask the big question or not. It's right there on the tip of my tongue, right next to my last forkful of fruit. I push a few grapes around my plate and take a chance.

"What made you quit?"

"I got pregnant. I wanted a baby, and your grandfather and I had been praying for a child. Once I found out I was pregnant, I then prayed that it would be a girl, you know, to carry on the Line."

I take another bite of my sandwich. "Well, I guess that prayer got answered."

Grandma giggles. "Yes, it did. Once your mother was born, I made a decision that I wanted to be home with her, shower her with love, teach her, and help her understand good choices from bad ones."

I'm gulping my iced tea, hurting for Grandma that

she threw away her opportunity to do something fantastic like the other Lauras.

"Do you ever regret not having some awesome career?"

Her eyes widen. "Oh, but I did have an awesome career! Raising a child is the biggest career any parent could ever have. I put your mother's birth certificate in the ledger behind my name. Do you know why?"

I shake my head, anxious to hear her answer.

"Because she is my greatest accomplishment. I'm so proud of her. And I'm not the first Laura to make motherhood a career. When Laura Ann and her husband moved to Texas, she became a full-time mom and raised Laura Jean right here on the farm."

I take another bite of my sandwich while I think about what Grandma just said. Sage's mother is a stay-at-home mom. Maybe she feels the same way. I just never thought of motherhood as a career. Grandma's talking to me about the pastor's sermon, but my mind is still on the shack. I accidentally interrupt her.

"I don't know if my classmates will understand the shack, Grandma. I mean, it's so much more than a slave shack. Do you realize every Laura in our Line has been in the shack, doing something? I've walked where they walked and stood where they stood."

Grandma nods as she smiles. "Isn't that a terrific feeling?"

I sigh. "It is, but I'm worried that when I get older, I won't be as good a Laura as the others. I don't want to be the worst Laura ever."

Grandma's face turns serious. "Baby Girl, you're going to do great things."

I shake my head. "But what if I fail? What if I get fired from my job? What if . . ."

She comes around the table and holds me close. "Then you'll fit right in with the rest of us. The ledger is full of failures as well as successes. If you study the ledger, you'll begin to see our legacy. Each of us fell down at some point in our lives. But we always got back up. As long as you get up more times than you fall down, you'll be a winner."

It's going to be easier than I ever thought possible telling Mrs. Jacobs she was right. That's because I'm more excited about the shack than any of the Lauras in the Line could ever be. And when my classmates come to the shack to check everything out, I'll stand there and watch them sneak looks at me and maybe even be jealous. But just when they think they've seen it all, I'll have them back away from the wall and introduce them to the bravest teenager ever.

chapter twenty-two

Maybe Troy will sit near me on the bus this morning and I'll tell him about my weekend. He'd be the only person in the whole school who might understand. And just knowing that he likes the Lauras and the shack makes a big difference.

When Troy gets on the bus, I smile as he walks my way.

"Hey, Troy."

"Hey."

He walks by me, and I turn around in my seat.

"Guess what I did this weekend."

He doesn't answer, and I take that as a no-guess.

"I finished the ledger, you know, inside the shack."

"Good for you."

The bus stops to pick up more students, but I keep talking to him.

"Yeah, it *was* good for me. Almost like a soap opera. I mean, Laura Elaine is a really cool Laura, but I think my favorite is . . ."

Troy looks around the bus at everyone staring at us, then hollers at me.

"Whatever, like I care!"

What the what? Did he just go off on me in front of all these people? Giggles and chuckles fill the bus as all eyes zoom in on me. I turn around and face the front, mouthing what I really want to say to Troy but don't because the words will get me kicked off the bus. Maybe he's not a morning person. Maybe he didn't have a good weekend. All I know is this rude dog attitude is getting old and I'm not going to put up with it much longer.

I'm so mad at him that it takes me a minute to realize that Sunny got on but Sage didn't. I wonder if she's okay. She didn't call me this weekend. I check my cell for missed calls. There's three. All from Sage. Oh, no.

I can't call her now because if the bus driver catches me using my cell, he's allowed to take it away and give it to the principal. Dang it.

Is she sick? Maybe she just wanted to talk. I could have told her about Laura Elaine.

Double dang it!

I can't even think of a good reason why I didn't check my cell. If something bad happened to her, I'll never forgive myself. What was I thinking? Maybe that's the problem. I didn't think of her at all this weekend. In my mind, the arrow on my Sage's-best-friend meter is pointing to THOUGHTLESS.

I get off the bus and dart to Sage's locker. I'm surprised but happy to see her standing there, even though she's surrounded by Pink Chips.

"Sage?"

She turns to me and I freeze. Her bangs are hot pink! Other students pass her, staring and pointing. She waves and they keep walking. Some chuckle, while others shake their heads. But Sage seems delighted with her new look.

"Laura, there you are." She rushes to me and the Pink Chips follow her.

"Where were you this weekend? I tried to call you, like, a thousand times."

I shrug, because it's too early in the morning to have all that Pink in my face. Plus I can't seem to come up with a good excuse. "My phone was off and I didn't realize it. Sorry."

Sunny smirks. "Who doesn't check their cell after

an hour of no calls or texts?"

Sage touches her bangs. "So what do you think?"

I can't tell her what I think. It could ruin our friendship, especially since I haven't been much of a best friend lately.

"It's a very pretty shade of pink."

She nods. "I got it done for my initiation today. Wait until you see my new outfit."

My eyebrows scrunch. "What initiation?"

The smile slides from Sage's face. Sunny rolls her eyes. London and Amanda jam their hands onto their hips and glare at my face. Sage steps closer to me.

"Today's my initiation, remember? In the shack."

Sweet Father of Forgotten Promises.

Sage sighs so hard that I know tears are next.

"Come on, Laura, don't do this to me. You promised."

I grab my head. "I've got so many things on my mind, Sage." I fake a smile, just to keep her calm. "Of course I didn't forget your big day. Let's work out the final details at lunch today."

I turn to Sunny and lose the smile. "Make it your business to find us. If you don't, the initiation and the *real* reason you're doing this are off."

Sunny flashes a smile. "I have no idea what you're talking about, Laura."

"That's probably true, since your brain is small

enough to stuff in a mosquito's ear and still have room for luggage."

Sage covers her mouth.

Sunny frowns. "We'll be at your pathetic lunch table today, and you better have the information I need to get the initiation done." She turns to Amanda and London.

"Leaving."

Sunny leads her girls down the center of the hallway. Even though it's crowded, students move to the sides to give the Royal Pink Chips their space. I watch them until they round the corner. A quick turn causes me to bump into Sage. She's staring at me.

"Oops! Sorry, Sage. I thought you'd left, too."

"What's going on, Laura? Have you found a new best friend? Just tell me."

"Huh? No!"

"Are you angry with me about something? Did I say something to hurt your feelings? Because if I did, I'm sorry."

"No, Sage, it's nothing like that. Look, I said I'll do it. Let's talk about it at lunch."

"You're not happy for me, are you?"

I hug her. "That's not it. I . . . I just don't feel comfortable about this! We'll talk, okay? Don't be mad at me. See you at lunch."

If I could pick a day to stay in bed, this would've been the day I chose. It started off horribly with Troy talking rude to me on the bus. Then I realized I missed three calls from Sage, and after seeing her pink bangs I bet one of those calls was for my opinion. But the worst brain drain has to be the initiation.

Last week, when Mrs. Jacobs announced the field trip, I wanted it canceled. Just thinking about my classmates climbing the steps to go inside that house of pain gave me ill-chills. But now I'm ready to give private tours, one classmate at a time if I could, just to make sure they understand that success runs in my blood and they can't hold me down.

The shack's not meant for stuff like initiations. That's just wrong.

Later, as I move through the cafeteria line, I grab my sorry salad with the weak dressing and a bottled water. Sage waves from across the room. I make my way to her table and take a seat. As usual, we've got the same horrible lunch.

"Okay, I'm all ears, Laura. Tell me what we have to do besides be careful. What else?"

I'm looking around the cafeteria when I see the Pink Chips heading our way.

Sunny grabs a chair and sits without being invited. "We're here. So what's the deal?"

I lean forward and talk softly. "What are you going

to make Sage do inside the shack?"

Sunny crosses her arms. "Her initiation is none of your business."

I don't back down. "I'm making it my business. Either fork over the plan or you can find another place for your initiation. And I know how badly you want to get into the shack."

Our eyes lock until Sunny caves. "She has to bring gifts. If we accept them, she's in."

I roll my eyes. "Fine. But I have to be in the shack during the initiation."

Sunny goes off. "No way! You're not a member, and this is private. Sage has to recite the secret Pink Chip motto. You can't be around for that."

Sage's eyes plead with me. I think of all the times she's helped me with stuff. I've got to figure out a way to make this work for her. So I lock in on Sunny again.

"Okay, here's how it's gonna go. You show up at five o'clock. You get thirty minutes. I'll be there for the initiation and I'll leave when Sage recites the motto. That's my final offer."

Sunny steps away from the table and huddles with London and Amanda while Sage stares at them. After an eternity, they come back and Sunny steps forward.

"We'll be there at five."

Sage grins at Sunny. "I won't be late. You're going to love my gifts."

Sunny returns a half grin. "Whatever."

But when she looks my way, her grin disappears. She stands, leans toward me, and whispers.

"No backing out, Fat Larda. If it's a real slave shack, the whole school is going to hear about it. Or I'll find out everything I need to know about that so-called storage shed."

I stab another piece of lettuce and point it at her.

"You don't have a clue about what you're going to see."

She jams her her hands on her hips. "Yes, I do. I know there's a bunch of embarrassing slavery stuff in there that you don't want anybody to see."

I scoot back and stand toe-to-toe with her, then drop the biggest fact she'll learn all day.

"You don't know doodly-squat." I turn to London and Amanda and mock Sunny:

"Leaving."

I grab my tray and walk away. Sunny yells at me. "You're done, Fat Larda!"

She passes me with London and Amanda following her. I stroll back to the table and take my seat across from Sage. But when I look at her, I realize this isn't close to being over. She's wiping her eyes with the sleeve of her blouse.

"I can't believe this is finally going to happen. We've been treated like trash for so long. Maybe we won't have to use that smelly bathroom that nobody else uses anymore. And maybe we won't have to walk against the wall when we change classes. We'll get respect!"

Sage wipes her face with her napkin. "Things are about to change for us, Laura. I don't care what they're going to make me do for initiation. I'm going to do it, for you, me, and anybody else who gets picked on for things they can't help. Once I become a Pink Chip, I'll stop all that ugly stuff Sunny does. And I think London will side with me."

She shakes her head. "I didn't know how much I'd been hurt until now."

I put my hand on hers. "The Pink Chips are getting an upgrade when they get you. Even though you probably don't believe me, I'm happy because you're happy."

"I know you don't like the Pink Chips. I totally get that you're doing this for me. You've put all your feelings aside so you could have my back. I've got a big surprise for them. They're going to love my gifts. I've been working on them since Sunny mentioned they were interested in me."

I'm barely listening to Sage, because I'm watching Sunny and her crew. But Sage pushes my tray and I turn her way. She's not crying anymore. Her face is dead red on mine. And even though she hasn't said anything, I feel like I need to answer her expression.

I lean forward. "What?"

She holds on to her water bottle. "Remember, this could be just as good for you as it is for me. She's got the power to change things, Laura. Whether you like Sunny or not, she can make the field trip go a lot easier. Her word is golden around here. That's not breaking news."

I lean back. "You don't understand, Sage. Things have already changed. And now what Sunny says or thinks is so not important."

Sage's eyebrows gather as she leans in. "What? What changed, Laura?"

I think of the letters and pictures, ribbons and recipes inside the ledger. And then the truth writes my problem across the center of my brain.

Even though I'm ready to open the doors of the shack, I'm not ready to share the Lauras.

Not even with my best friend. Or my worst enemy.

All the way home from school, I'm thinking how I'm going to get Grandma to buy into this initiation thing. She probably won't. I bet she just flat out says no. I can hear the television on in the living room. The crack of the bat and a "That's outta here!" yell from Grandma tells me how she's spending her afternoon. I wonder what she did *before* she learned the game. I pull up next to her chair, bend down, and give her a hug.

"Hey, Grandma, looks like a good game."

"The Rangers and the Indians. Doesn't that sound like a good cowboy movie?"

I laugh with her and agree before asking the ultimate question.

"I invited a few girls over to see the shack today. Is that okay?"

She perks up. "Oh, wonderful! I'm so happy to know that you're having a little girl gathering to introduce your friends to the Line. That just warms my heart."

I nod. "So, they'll be here around five. We'll be finished in half an hour or sooner, okay?"

Grandma starts to get up. "I'll make a caramel cake for you and your friends."

I put my hand on her shoulder. "No! I mean, no thanks, Grandma. These girls eat nothing but raw vegetables. Can you imagine?"

Grandma stares at me with her mouth wide open. "No."

I smile and nod. "I know, right? Anyway, we're going to talk, you know, girlie stuff. But my friends might stop talking if a grown-up comes in."

She giggles. "I remember those days. And you're right, they probably will clam up. So I'll wait on you to come back to the house, okay?"

"Thanks, Grandma. Can I take a few chairs from the kitchen out to the shack?"

"Sure! Have fun!"

This is the second lie I've told in a week. And both of them have to do with the shack. But this has got to be the worst ever. I lied to Grandma, and I'm sure the arrow on my good-granddaughter meter reads . . . BROKEN.

chapter twenty-three

I stand outside and check my watch. It's just a few minutes before five. Suddenly, I notice Sage's brother Kevin's white truck heading up the hill. There's a pink car behind it. Seriously? A pink car? It has to be them.

Sage gets out of the truck, and her brother hands her two huge shopping bags.

When the Pink Chips get out of the car, I can't help but ask.

"How did you get a pink car to ride around in?"

London smiles. "My mom sells Mary Kay cosmetics."

I'm not sure what that has to do with a pink car,

but I just nod and let it go. Sage is sporting a brand-new outfit with a new necklace and earrings. I rub her arm.

"You look runway ready, Sage. Dark blue is a good color for you."

She's misting and breathing short breaths. "Thanks, Laura."

I reach for one of her bags.

"Just relax. Let me help you with those."

Sunny steps in between us. "She doesn't need any help. Sage has to carry everything she brought with her, and she also has to clean up and carry everything out that she brought."

I frown. "Why? Her initiation hasn't started yet."

Sunny glares at me. "Yes it has."

When Sunny says those three words, something burns in my gut. I try to ignore it and stay strong for Sage, because this is her big moment. When Sunny moves from between us, I mouth to her *Good luck.* She smiles back and mouths *Thanks.*

I'll never tell her what's going on inside me right now. She wouldn't understand. Helping with Sage's initiation is like Grandma giving me a plateful of Almond Joys for breakfast. She knows that's what I want, but it's not good for me.

I'm ready for this to be over. So I try to add some of Dad's bass in my voice, just to let them know I mean business. I point and walk.

"Let's go."

I lead them across the grass where the ground is soft. Sunny and Amanda complain about their heels getting stuck in the dirt. I pretend I don't hear them. London's walking with Sage, bringing up the rear. A window opens and Grandma shouts out at us.

"Hi there! I hope y'all enjoy yourselves! Oh, hi, Sage! I didn't know you were coming, too! What's that pink stuff in your hair? That's not gum, is it?"

Sage returns the wave. "No, it's just . . . I was having some fun, that's all."

"Okay. Well, enjoy the shack. Don't forget to check out the Laura Line."

I hear Sunny whisper. "The what?"

I wave and smile at Grandma, hoping she'll stop talking. I didn't want them to know about the crosses. Now they'll want to see them. I just know it.

Sage and the Pink Chips aren't the only ones weighing me down. The Lauras are heavy on my mind.

And the cherry on top of this pile of problems is I lied to Grandma. I look over my shoulder to see if she's still looking our way from her kitchen window. She waves.

I pick up the pace. "Come on!"

Soon, everyone's standing in front of the shack.

Silence.

I'm not telling them jack. And I don't think the Lauras would care much about these snooty booty rich patooty girls anyway. But then Sage opens her mouth.

"There's a cemetery in the backyard. Wanna see it?"

I open up a conversation in Eye-ish to Sage. She sends two eyeballfuls of apology my way, and I accept it as we walk around back.

London gets close. "They're all named Laura?"

I can't resist. "You're actually looking at the Laura Line."

Amanda turns to me. "Were they all in the military or something?"

"So what's the deal with this cemetery, Larda?" I can tell Sunny's curious.

I walk up to her. "The name's Laura. Don't disrespect the Line."

Sunny walks away. "Whatever. Let's get this over with."

We all turn to walk back to the shack. London's still walking the Line, looking at each cross, touching the wood. Since she's the only Pink Chip I really like, I don't say anything. But Sunny calls out to her.

"London!"

Once we're all in front of the shack, I speak to the group.

"Listen, the stuff in here is worth more than you'll earn in your whole life. Don't make me regret letting you use it."

Sage speaks up, gripping her two bags and grinning. "You rock, Laura."

I stay focused. "Let's go inside."

They follow me. London has moved to the front of the line, and I hear her gasp behind me when she steps inside. She checks out pictures as the others move around, touching and looking at Laura Jean's old-time sewing machine and Laura Elaine's typewriter.

London points to a picture. "Who's this?"

I walk over to the wall. "That's Laura Jean. She was a model. On Friday, during the field trip, my grandma will answer all the questions you ask. Okay, let's get started. The little chair is off-limits, so don't sit on it."

I park near the door and the Pink Chips gather around the table.

Sage opens her bags and takes out a jug of Hawaiian Punch, five plastic cups, and five plates. She opens a box and puts a pink cookie on each plate and then pours each of us a glass of punch. I wink at her as she hands me mine. Then, she makes the big announcement.

"Now for the megagift."

She reaches into her second bag and gives Sunny a pink binder with her name in gold glitter on the cover. She does the same for Amanda and London. They open their binders, and smiles blossom all over the room. Sage starts with Sunny and explains her gift as Sunny looks through the pages.

"I took that picture of you while you were listening to one of our guest speakers in the auditorium. And that one I took at the baseball game. This is a picture from last year during the Spring Dance. I found it in some old film that didn't get used."

Sage goes on and on about Sunny's picture book and then moves on to Amanda, then London, doing the same thing.

As the Pink Chips enjoy their pictures, I give Sage a thumbs-up. She gives me one back and then asks, "Do you like my gifts?"

Sunny closes her binder and eyeballs her Chipmates. They all nod and Sunny responds.

"We accept your initiation gifts. Have you memorized the Pink Chip motto?"

Sage rubs her hands together. "I sure have, and I'm ready to recite it."

Sunny stands. "Good. Okay, ladies, help me find something to cover that window. Oh, there's a basket of blankets on the floor over there. We can use those. Lard . . . Laura, you have to leave."

I tilt my head. "You didn't say anything about covering the window, Sunny."

She shrugs. "I didn't know the shack had one. You can't hear or watch Sage recite the motto. Will you at least help us put the blanket up?"

Something's wrong about this. I feel it in my knower. Reluctantly, I go against my feelings and help put the blanket up anyway. Sunny goes outside and then comes back in.

"Nope, can't see a thing through the window from out there. Okay, Laura, you can leave now. We'll be finished in a few minutes."

I look at my watch. "You've got five minutes left."

Sage waves at me. "Thanks, Laura."

I sit on the step for what feels like an eternity. Finally I get up and try to see what's going on through the window. I move around, hoping to find a crack in the wood so I can peek inside.

My thoughts jumble as my heart thumps faster. My knower's going berserk, and I'm tempted to crash the party. Instead, I holler inside to them.

"Two more minutes."

I close my eyes and try to listen, but instead my mind shows me a woman sitting in the grass listening to children read. Suddenly their books close and blow away. It's Laura Mae. I know it. What's happening? Is she trying to tell me something?

I call out to Sage. "Is everything okay?"

I keep looking for that crack in the wood, hoping

I can see inside, but all I hear is a chant.

I close my eyes again. This time, Laura Jean comes to me. She's celebrating a dress she finished on her sewing machine. It's beautiful, with tiny pearls around the hem and neckline.

My eyelids flip open. Oh, no! Laura Jean's sewing machine is still on the floor! I forgot to move it! I begin to holler at the top of my lungs.

"Time's up. Hey, what's going on in there?"

My eyes go wide when Laura Elaine's eulogy appears in my head.

I stop breathing because the ledger is still on the table. My legs move automatically as my chest tightens at the thought of what could be happening to the pages of the ledger. Oh, no . . .

"I'm coming in!"

I hear Sage, screaming something at the top of her lungs. There's laughter, but to me, there's nothing funny about this situation.

All I can think about are the Lauras. They're watching. Something's wrong. I can feel it. Sadness creeps over me, and I'm sure it's coming from them. Just as I reach the door,

CRACK! BOOM-BOOM-MA-BOOM!

"SAGE!!!"

chapter twenty-four

Sage's body lies flat around pieces of wood. She's trying to get up but can't. The Pink Chips stand in shock, staring at her and the broken chair.

The broken chair . . .

I check the table, hoping that it was one of the regular chairs, not the little one. Not the little uneven one.

Please. Not the chair Grandma sat in as a child.

Not that one.

"Laura!"

And at that very moment, I lose my balance. The room's spinning.

I know Sage is calling my name, saying something to me, but everything seems unreal, like it's one of my daydreams. I grab the edge of the table, trying to sit, when my eyes catch a glistening color coming from the center of the table.

No.

It's the ledger, with spilled punch all over the cover.

I point at the gravel road and scream.

"Get out! NOW!"

Sage gets to her feet. "Laura, I'm sorry. I was almost finished reciting the motto, and the chair broke while I was standing on it. I'll clean it up."

Heat rushes to my face. "You were standing on it?"

"You said we couldn't *sit* on it. I didn't think . . . I'm sorry, Laura. It was an accident. Look . . . we're almost finished."

I snap at her, "No, you're finished right now!"

Silence.

Sunny walks toward the door. "Leaving."

On her way out, Sage puts her arm on my shoulder. "I didn't think it would break."

Amanda follows here. "I hope you can fix it . . . Laura."

London's the saddest of all. She's picking up pieces of the chair.

I can't take it. "Just leave it, London."

She slowly walks to the door, then rushes back to the pink car.

But it's Sage who surprises me the most when she hollers at me.

"You don't even like this place! You're ruining everything! I was almost finished!"

I holler back at her. "Then take it to your house, Sage! And I don't care if you're mad!"

Now she's crying. "Why do you care so much about a silly little chair? I thought you hated this shack?"

I begin to cry too. "I did. But . . . but . . . that chair belonged to . . . Just go!"

Sage gives me a long look before rushing out to catch up with the others.

I close the door and use my blouse to dab the punch off the ledger. As I'm dabbing, I notice Laura Jean's sewing machine turned over. I step over the broken chair and put it back in its place next to the typewriter.

That's as far as I make it. I sit on the floor next to the broken chair and burst into tears. Sage is right. What *was* I thinking? How am I going to fix this chair before Grandma sees it? Is that punch going to stain the ledger?

I need the earth to open and swallow me.

Knock, knock, knock.

I scream from the floor. "Go away!"

"It's me. Sage."

"Leave me alone!"

The door creaks. "I'm so sorry, Laura."

"Just go away, Sage. Your precious Pink Chips are waiting for you."

She sits on the floor next to me. "No, they're not. I told them to leave. I caused all this drama. I can't let you take the blame, Laura."

Her sniffles come quickly. "Even if it means I'm back to being Sage the Submarine."

The pain in this room is overwhelming. The air is so thick, I can barely breathe. I've never heard Sage cry so hard, and there's no signs of her stopping. As I inhale hot air, hotter tears sizzle down my face.

Suddenly, I see a pair of house shoes at the door. Seconds later, a cake falls in slow motion.

SPLAT!

"Baby Girl?"

I hate that name. And I didn't realize it until now. Baby Girl sounds so childish and innocent and pretty and . . . and not guilty. I can't look up.

"What happened in here? Why is the blanket over the window?"

Grandma reaches down and picks up a piece of the broken wood.

She glances at the table, then back at me. "This

isn't the chair my daddy made for me, is it? No . . . it can't . . ."

"Grandma . . ." She stumbles, just like I did, and reaches for the table's edge. Still staring at the splintered wood sprawled across the floor, Grandma plops in a chair and is about to say something when she notices the ledger on the table. She drops the wood, reaches out, wipes her hand across the cover, and looks at the wet red stain on her palm.

Her heavy sobs break me down. I lean to the floor and curl up like an infant. Sage gets up and runs out the door, leaving me with Grandma. We're crying in the shack together, both for different reasons. But Grandma's reasons hurt me so bad that I've got to try and explain myself. So I sit up and talk through my own tears.

"See . . . Sunny said they just wanted to use the shack for Sage's initiation. Sage promised nothing would happen and they'd be careful. I tried to watch everything, but at the last minute, they asked me to leave."

Grandma's still crying, wiping the spilled punch from the ledger onto her blouse. It looks like blood, and I feel like I'm dying.

"I've let you down. I've let the whole Laura Line down."

Grandma's crying slows to sniffles as she picks up that piece of wood again.

"This table and chairs came from Laura Belle. And this ledger came from Laura Mae. Laura Belle and Laura Ann rode in a horse-drawn carriage all the way from Harlem, New York, just to put this dining room table and chairs in here. It was in Laura Belle's restaurant."

My belly rumbles. Things are crashing around internally. This isn't some little stomach storm brewing. I'm shattering into pieces much smaller than Grandma's broken chair.

Another apology would be weak as water, and I'm too embarrassed to even say it again.

There's nobody to blame but me. I get off the floor and make a promise.

"I'm going to fix it, Grandma. You'll see. I'll fix everything."

chapter twenty-five

Sage comes back inside the shack. Her face is streaky red as she walks by me and speaks directly to Grandma.

"Mrs. Anderson, please don't blame Laura. I broke the chair. Laura was just trying to help me with something I wanted more than anything. I'll bring all my savings to you tomorrow. Maybe we can find another chair."

Grandma gets up. "I don't want your money, sweetheart. This isn't about money. I need to lie down. Baby Girl, wake me in an hour and I'll make dinner."

I nod because the lump in my throat won't let me

talk. I swallow hard, reach out, and touch Grandma. She stops, and I look at the chair piece she's got cradled in her hand.

"Grandma, I need to keep all the wood together."

She hands it to me on her way out as Sage picks up more stray pieces from the floor.

"She hates me, doesn't she?"

I shake my head. "If she's going to hate anybody, it's going to be me."

Now Sage is crying again, and I can't take it. I'm barely holding on myself as I lean against the wall of pictures, wishing Sage would just go home. It's not that I don't want help, it's just . . . I can't. I'm on overload. So I close my eyes and hope she disappears.

But she keeps talking.

"All I've thought about for the last week is finally being somebody other than Sage the Submarine or Sumo Sage. I wanted this so badly, Laura. And now I'm back to being just . . . you know."

Yeah . . . I know. Fat Larda is the name I've been strapped with, and I hate it. But I've never felt desperate to change the way Sage does. And I never knew why until I read the ledger. Not one of the Lauras let her weight keep her from doing anything she wanted to do. Not even Laura Ann. I open my eyes and stare at the pictures of the Laura Line. I keep my eyes on them and signal to Sage.

"Come here. I want to show you something."

She comes over to the wall. "I've already seen these, Laura."

I keep staring at them. "Really? Then I'm going to ding you for not paying attention. Look at them closely, Sage. They all have something in common."

Sage lets out a big sigh. "Okay, let's see . . . they're all women. They're all African American. They're all fat. Are you trying to make me feel worse?"

I shake my head. "No. I'm trying to make a point. *You* see fat. Look at their faces. They're all smiling. They're all happy. And they're showing off something they're good at."

Sage is really studying them, so I keep talking.

"Are you a Pink Chip? Did you pass their initiation? Those pictures you gave them were amazing. To me, there's no reason why they wouldn't take you."

Sage stares at the floor. "They told me they were going to think about it and let me know. Sunny said I might have to do another initiation, so maybe I should start taking more pictures of them to put together another gift for that."

I point to a picture of Laura Elaine. Then I pull Sage to the table, open up the soggy ledger cover, and show her one of Laura Elaine's news articles.

"She was a news reporter back in the day when

they didn't want women, and I bet there weren't many full-figured African American women in the newsroom either. But she made them want her. Laura Elaine made her boss see past all the other stuff. He saw her talent."

Sage stares at the article as if it's a piece of gold. She runs her fingers over the plastic, just like I did. Watching her is like watching myself try to get my head around what I was really seeing. But I'm not finished. I pull Sage away from the table.

"And that typewriter on the floor, that's what she used to type that article. And it even had a broken key. The letter G doesn't work."

Sage stares at the typewriter. "What?"

"And that's what you did to the Pink Chips. Don't you see? Even though they may have been trying to use you to get free pictures, you got the best deal out of the whole thing. Now you know people can see your talent, which means they're not looking at your weight."

"You think so?"

"Heck to the double yes."

From the window, I see Sage's brother's truck. She heads for the door.

"You're my best friend, Laura."

"Yes, I am."

She looks around. "And we were wrong about this place. It's . . . beyond amazing."

I smile sadly. "Yeah, it is. See you tomorrow."

I grab her sleeve. "Wait." Then I put my hand on her shoulder. She puts her hand on mine and says what we both need to hear.

"I will always . . ."

I nod. ". . . have your back."

As I walk Sage to her brother's truck, I notice Grandma inching toward her car. Each step she takes seems painful. I wave good-bye to Sage and rush to her.

"Grandma, where are you going?"

Her face is swollen. "I called Edna. She wants me to come over."

I've never been to a teacher's house before, and I know it's got to be a punishable crime in the unwritten handbook for students.

I don't care. I open up the passenger door and slide onto the seat. I refuse to look at Grandma. I feel her staring at me, waiting for me to say something else, but I don't. Finally, she starts the car and we're on our way.

There's no conversation between us, and I'm okay with that. I've got enough things on my mind to have a thousand conversations with myself. As I stare out of the window, I realize that I've only been on the farm for nine measly days. In that time, I've been through a lot, but a few things stand out more than others.

1. My history teacher is my grandma's BFF.
2. Troy lives down the road from my grandma, cuts her grass, and knew about the shack and the Laura Line.
3. My grandma loves me enough to learn something new, just because it's something I like to do.
4. The slave shack needs a name change. It's so much more than that.
5. The Laura Line isn't just a line of crosses.

Even though those are big-time things to learn in just a short amount of time, my mind can't shake what happened today. Grandma's hurting, and it's my fault for being careless. I've got to figure out how to make this right. I sure hope Mrs. Jacobs has some ideas. And I hope she doesn't try to go all crazy on me in front of Grandma. I feel bad enough.

Mrs. Jacobs doesn't live far from Royal Middle School. It's an old neighborhood with one-story houses, small front yards, and cars parked on the street. Even though I knew this subdivision existed, I'd never been in it until now.

Grandma pulls up behind Mrs. Jacobs's black Jeep

Cherokee and I'm suddenly terrified. My legs feel like concrete, and I'm thinking maybe this wasn't a good move on my part. I could sit in the car and wait for Grandma to finish talking. How long could that take?

Then Grandma taps my shoulder. "Baby Girl, I know you didn't do anything on purpose. I'm hurt more that you didn't tell me the truth about what was really going on in the shack. But I'm proud of you for wanting to take responsibility. That's what a Laura would do."

I'm ready to cry again. Even though I've done absolutely nothing to fix what happened, just knowing Grandma doesn't hate me energizes me even more to make things right.

We open our doors, get out of the car, and walk hand in hand to Mrs. Jacobs's house. She opens her door and hugs Grandma for a long time. Finally she lets go and moves aside. "Come on in. I've made some dinner. Have you eaten yet?"

I answer for both of us. "We haven't."

It smells like fresh-baked bread and muscle ointment inside. Even though it's a warm April evening, her house feels like it's July. Then I notice her furniture has plastic covers on it.

"Is this new furniture?"

She shakes her head. "Oh, no, I've had that set for over ten years."

It's a matching sofa and chair set with tigers, lions, and leopards in a safari scene. I feel sorry for them with all that plastic covering across their faces. They must feel like they got sentenced to the worst zoo ever.

The wooden coffee and end tables have carved faces of African warriors with spears and tribal headdresses. By the way her house is set up, I'm expecting Tarzan and Cheeta to swing through at any moment.

"Come on in and have a seat," she says.

I don't know why I'm stunned that her kitchen is decorated in red and white. I was expecting something more . . . historical. Instead it seems Mrs. Jacobs has a thing for roosters.

Her coffee pot is a rooster. When it's tilted, coffee pours from its beak.

Ew.

Her oven mitts and dish towels are white with big red rooster faces in the middle.

What the what?

Even her cookie jar is a rooster. The head comes off and you have to reach down its neck to grab a cookie.

That's just nasty.

"Laura, would you like a glass of milk or iced tea?"

"Tea, please."

After pouring me a glass, Mrs. Jacobs opens her refrigerator and pulls out a beautiful fruit salad. Once it's on the table, she rubs her hands together.

"I've got all kinds of delicious things for us to eat."

Grandma moves her fruit around the plate with her fork. I'm stabbing a piece of green melon when a smell I'm not used to trespasses up my nose.

I have to ask. "What's that smell?"

"Black-eyed peas with sage sausage. I made some rice to go under it. And biscuits."

I get more fruit. That's where I'll live today, because I don't eat anything with the word eyes in it, and sage sausage reminds me of Sage and all the drama I've got right now.

But Grandma grabs an ice-cream scooper and scoops rice into a bowl. Then she tops it with a massive helping of those black-eyed peas. I don't have a problem with it until she shoves the bowl next to me with a biscuit on the side.

"It's important that you try this, Baby Girl. I think you'll like it a lot."

Then she touches my arm. "Taste them. For me, okay?"

After all the drama I caused her, tasting a bowl of black-eyed peas is the least I can do. I shovel up half a spoonful of them. Even though I'm not looking, I can feel the eyes in those peas staring at me. Okay, here goes.

This . . . wait . . . Mmmm.

Grandma and Mrs. Jacobs make small talk, but soon Mrs. Jacobs turns to me.

"So what happened today?"

Grandma shifts her eyes my way. This is it. The polite time is over. But no matter how Mrs. Jacobs responds, it can't hurt any more than I'm already hurting.

I tell her.

chapter twenty-six

Grandma's quiet while I empty my most shameful moments on the table for Mrs. Jacobs to hear. I tell her how embarrassed I've been in history class because I don't understand how African Americans allowed a whole other race to make them slaves and do all of their chores.

I told her the last thing I ever wanted to do was come live on the farm because I absolutely hated the shack. I didn't know why my family still had something so cruel, and to me, there's no excuse for an African American family to have a slave shack on their property.

And then she scheduled the field trip, and I had to do something to get it canceled for good.

Mrs. Jacobs's forehead wrinkles. "Well, you may have succeeded. I don't know if your grandmother will ever feel comfortable letting people inside the shack again."

I shake my head. "Please let me finish. After I went in the shack for the first time, I felt strange but I shook it off. I fought *liking* it. I even told myself that it was just an ugly, useless slave shack. But I knew inside that it was more than that. And the ledger proved it."

Mrs. Jacobs leans forward. "So you *did* read all of the ledger?"

My head droops and I stare at my lap. "You win, Mrs. Jacobs. I found that 'one amazing' thing you knew was there all along. I got to know them. I even walked inside the shack like I think Laura Jean would have walked in one of her dresses. It wasn't until the chair broke and the ledger got wet that I realized what I'd done. By then, it was too late."

Mrs. Jacobs scoots back from the table. "Oh, my heavens! The ledger's damaged too?"

A tear rolls down Grandma's face. I want to explain better, but I can't find the words. Then, without realizing it, Mrs. Jacobs throws me a lifeline.

"Laura, you're telling me that you didn't want your classmates inside the shack, yet you allowed an initiation to take place in it? I don't understand."

It's time to stretch my legs and walk this one out. So I get up from the table and walk around the kitchen as I talk.

"I made a promise, Mrs. Jacobs. First, I was doing my best friend a favor by allowing the initiation to take place. After I started hanging out with the Lauras, I wanted to cancel the whole initiation thing, but I couldn't because I had made a promise to Sage. As a member of the Laura Line, I wasn't about to go back on my word."

I lean against the refrigerator and look out the kitchen window at Mrs. Jacobs's backyard. There's no cemetery. It doesn't look like there's anything super-special back there. I wonder if she even understands how I feel. I turn to look directly at her.

"Then the little chair broke, and I knew those girls would never understand what they had done. I wanted them out. At that moment, I felt they were trespassing, disrespecting the Lauras . . . and the shack."

I'm walking again, trying to figure out exactly what I want to say.

"I mean, I know each one of the Lauras' histories, and I feel as if they know me. That doesn't make sense because they're dead, but there's a connector or something."

Grandma lifts her coffee toward me. "It makes

perfect sense to me."

I keep talking. "I realized I'd made a major mistake. I ran inside the shack and told the girls to leave. And now, I'm the worst Laura ever. Even worse than Laura Ann."

Coffee shoots from Grandma's lips. She wipes her mouth and laughs.

"Baby Girl, that just made me think of something. Did you know Laura Ann . . ."

I grin. ". . . threw a baseball? Is that the coolest thing or what? But Laura Ann and Pierre? Don't even go there, Grandma."

Now Mrs. Jacobs giggles. "We talk about Laura Ann all the time. She was a piece of work, wasn't she?"

Now we're laughing, talking about Laura Ann and widening our conversation to include some of the other Lauras. Eventually, I ease my way out of the conversation, tiptoe over to the stove, and get some more of those black-eyed peas. But Grandma busts me.

"So you like those peas, huh?"

I nod and sit back in my chair. "Mrs. Jacobs, where'd you learn how to make this dish?"

"It's Laura Belle's. Your grandma was kind enough to share this one with me."

My mind drifts back to the newspaper article about Laura Belle's restaurant. How people came from everywhere to eat her good cooking. It's easy to believe these peas and sausage were a big hit. And she left the recipe for us. I have to speak up.

"Mrs. Jacobs, you may not believe me, but I'm more proud of that shack and the Laura Line than I ever thought I could be. But I'm so scared that one of my classmates may break something else. I want them to see it, but they don't care like I do."

Grandma reaches for my hand. "How can you make them care, Laura Eboni?"

Her eyes are locked on mine, almost staring through them, as if speaking to something deeper than what she sees. I can't unlock that eye grip she's got on me as she speaks again.

"We must always do what's best for the Line. It doesn't matter about what we want, only what's best for the Lauras."

And with that, I know what I need to do. "Okay. The field trip's on. But instead of Grandma giving the tour, I'm going to give it."

Mrs. Jacobs chimes in. "Splendid! I knew you'd find something in the ledger that you'd consider amazing. What did you find?

I look from Mrs. Jacobs to Grandma and then back to Mrs. Jacobs again.

"I found me."

Mrs. Jacobs grins. *"Magnifica, Señorita."*

chapter twenty-seven

Tuesday at school, I try to lie low, but it seems as if every person in the hall stops me.

"Is there really a slave shack on your grandmother's farm?"

"Uh-huh."

That's all they get. I don't offer any more 4-1-1 than that. I know it's Sunny spreading the word. But the weirdest thing happens on my way to lunch. I spot Troy coming down the hall. I usually stare at him until he's completely out of sight, and today is no different except for one thing. As he passes by, he nods.

"What's up, Dyson?"

What the what?

And I can't think of what to say back. It's pitiful. Just a few days ago, if Troy had spoken to me in the hall at school, I would have fixed my hair, redone my lip gloss, and popped a breath mint before saying, "Oh, nothing."

But now, my love for Troy is on hold. I've got big-time heavy-hitter-type stuff to handle, and I only have a few days to get it done.

In history class, I take my seat and bury my face in my book. When the bell rings, Mrs. Jacobs closes the door.

"Take your seats."

Moments later, she paces around the front of the class.

"Any permission slips for the field trip on Friday?"

I raise my hand. Mrs. Jacobs comes to my desk, and I hand her the crumpled-up permission slip with Grandma's signature. She doesn't say a word.

Sunny and London both raise their permission slips in the air. I'm sure they're coming just to try to trash the place again, but I won't be fooled like I was last time.

London looks my way, then raises her hand again.

"Mrs. Jacobs, I've already been to the shack."

If looks could kill, London would be dead in her seat. Mrs. Jacobs crosses her arms over her chest and stands in front of London's desk. She doesn't look happy.

"Is there something else you want to tell us, London?"

I know Mrs. Jacobs is looking for a confession. That's not what she gets.

"Yeah, I want to say that the shack on Larda's . . . I mean Laura's grandmother's farm totally surprised me. It's . . . it's . . . I can't wait to go inside again."

London looks my way, and I give her a quick smile. Random talk about the field trip starts, and it gets so loud that Mrs. Jacobs has to make everybody settle down.

Mrs. Jacobs cuts her eyes my way. Her eyebrows rise. My shoulders lower. I don't know what to say or think. Most of all, I just want to hang out in the shack and talk to the Lauras about how to fix that chair. That's the most important thing to me right now.

Later that afternoon, I leave the door open to the shack and crack the window, just in case there's any Pink Chip smell lingering. I need to work on this chair, but I don't even know where to start. There's a basket full of tiny broken pieces. I'm not even sure which piece goes where. I rip open an Almond Joy while I think about it. As I chew, instead of thinking about how to fix the chair, I realize I've only got two Almond Joys left. And now I'm really bummed.

"Hey!"

I almost jump out of my skin, but once I see Troy looking in the window at me, I can't help but smile.

"What are you doing here? It's only Tuesday."

"We got a new customer. They want their yard done tomorrow, so Dad got your grandma's okay to switch days just for this week." He stares at the basket of wood, then looks at the table.

"What the heck happened in here?"

I tell him the story, and he's shaking his head and spitting in the grass.

"So the rumor *was* true. I can't believe you let Sunny and the rest of those Potato Chips in the shack. I mean, they don't care about anything but themselves."

I bite my lip to keep my laugh inside my mouth. "Did you say Potato Chips?"

Troy folds his arms across his chest. "That's what I said, and I ain't taking it back."

I let out a big sigh. "Grandma's really upset about it and . . . well, I don't feel very good either. I've got to get this fixed."

Troy comes inside and grabs a piece of the wood out of the basket. He doesn't move when I step closer to him to see what he's looking at. I guess he's used to me now. He turns the wood over a few times like he's some kind of expert. He even sniffs it.

"Yeah, they busted it up pretty good. It's going to be hard fixing it."

Troy steps out of the shack and picks up his sprayer. He's back to spraying the garden when his cell rings. I sit in a chair near the window, just to find out if it's a girl calling him.

He puts the phone on speaker so he can talk and spray the flowers at the same time.

Troy: "Yo."

Shane: "Whatcha' doing?"

Troy: "Hey, what's up, bro?"

Shane: "Just got the new MLB for Xbox. Want to come over? Where are you?"

Troy: "I'm with my dad on a job."

Shane: "Are you near my house?"

Troy: "No. Remember I told you we cut Larda's grandma's grass?"

As he says that, Troy's eyes go high beam and meet with mine. I'm zoned in on him, and he closes the cell without saying good-bye to Shane. But the damage is done. I feel the heat rising inside me, even as he tries to explain.

"I didn't mean to say that."

Low-down dirty dog. "But you said it."

Troy frowns. "Well, you shouldn't have been eavesdropping on my business!"

Silence.

He sighs and lowers his head. "I didn't mean that, either. I'm sorry, Dyson."

His apologies are becoming weaker than that see-through salad dressing I drizzle on my salad every day at lunch. I stay in my seat, hold on to the windowsill, stick my head out the window, and let him have it.

"You don't have to apologize to me, Troy Bailey, because really, all the Fat Larda remarks and the cruel stuff you say about me with Shane and your other friends—I'm sick of it!"

He tries to interrupt me. "Wait, Dyson—"

Grass-cutting, liver-lipped alien. "And all the eavesdropping you do on conversations my grandma has with your dad about the Laura Line is lame."

He puts up a finger. "Hold on a minute—"

I've got my finger *and* my neck working now. "Heck to the infinite no I won't hold on a minute! You're the one who seems to be all in *my* business. While you're around here growing flowers and stuff, why don't you grow some business of your own!"

I'm going off the deep end when he reaches through the window and touches my hand. My anger gets shed like a useless layer of skin. Orchestra music plays, and the clouds seem to move in rhythm. My lips pooch and my face relaxes, just in case I'm about to get a kiss. But instead, his face softens, and he looks more sincere than I've ever seen before.

"I swear that slipped, Dyson. I'm really trying to stop calling you Larda, because I just don't want to anymore. You're not that girl."

"Then what girl am I?"

He spits in the grass and takes his hand off mine. "I don't know! Don't you know? I mean, you taught me how to throw a curveball. I struck out two guys with that pitch yesterday. And you're part of the Laura Line. You're not fake like the Pink Chips. You're just . . . different."

It's about time he got a clue. We're making progress, and I can't wait for him to get down on one knee and ask me to be his girl. It'll happen.

I sigh and shrug. "Anyway, I've got to figure out what to do about this broken chair."

Troy shrugs. "Why don't you ask Mrs. Jacobs? She knows all kinds of stuff."

Of course! Why didn't I think of her before? I could kiss Troy, but instead, I grin.

"Great idea, Bailey. Want a quick lesson on how to throw a nasty changeup?"

He drops his watering can and jogs toward the mound. "Heck yeah!"

chapter twenty-eight

That evening, I send Mrs. Jacobs an email and she replies:

> This may be a good time for your grandma to reconsider making the shack a historical monument. Go to the Texas Historical Commission (it's down the street from the public library) and speak to a man named Mr. Bob Adams. He's already got a file started on the shack. I'll call him and let him know you're coming. Good luck, Laura.

The next day after school I rush to catch the Main Street metro bus. It stops right in front of the library, and that's where I get off. Just a short walk down the street puts me where I need to be. I open the door to the Texas Historical Commission office. There's a man with curly black hair standing at the front desk with three women.

"Are you Laura?"

I nod. "Mr. Adams?"

"That's me. Come on back to my office and let's have a little chitchat."

Click.

A short gate releases, and Mr. Adams pushes it open. "Would you like something to drink?"

I walk quickly through the gate. "No, thank you. I don't have much time before the last bus leaves."

Mr. Adams replies, "Have a seat. Mrs. Jacobs called me this morning and told me you would be stopping by. I pulled the file on the Anderson property. Let's see, my notes say there's a slave shack and a cemetery. How can I help you, Laura?"

I slouch in the chair. "Something got broken in the shack, a very important chair, and I can't fix it myself. So I was wondering if you could send a repair person out to the shack to do it. See, my grandma doesn't have a lot of memories with her mom, just the ones that took place in the shack. And now, without that chair . . . can you help me?"

Mr. Adams clears his throat. "I'm sorry about the accident, Laura. I can tell it was not just important to your grandma, but to you, too."

I wipe mist from my forehead. "My class is making a field trip to the shack, and it just wouldn't be the same without the chair. I mean how am I going to talk about Grandma when she was a little girl and how she sat in that chair and the chair isn't there?"

Mr. Adams nods. "Let's see, I know of a few organizations that may be willing to help you with that, but first things first. I don't have any pictures of the shack or the cemetery. I also need pictures of any letters, maps, antiques . . ."

I sit up. "I can get that."

Mr. Adams hands me his business card. "Great. I'd also like to have information on why this shack is so special. I'll need proof of its history."

I sit up straighter. "I can get that, too!" I reach into my backpack and pull out a map I made especially for him and place it on his desk.

"Mr. Adams, you could come see the shack for yourself if you wanted. And maybe even bring that repair person with you. Because, see, this Friday, I'm giving the first ever tour of the shack and the cemetery. I made you a map of how to get to our farm. But you could MapQuest it if you wanted. The address is right there, and that's my cell number."

He puts the map in the file. "Thanks for the map, Laura, but unfortunately, I can't make the tour. I've got a meeting in Austin on Friday. And besides, it will be impossible to have anything fixed by then. That's just not enough time. Plus there's lots of paperwork that needs to be filled out, and I need signatures and . . . you understand?"

I slouch again. "I guess so. Thanks, anyway, Mr. Adams."

As I head toward the door, he calls out to me, "Don't give up, Laura. You've got to start somewhere. And call me if you have any questions. My number's on the card."

I'm calling Grandma to ask her to pick me up where the city bus drops me off, since it's about two miles from the farm, when a horn honks. It's Sage and her brother. He pulls over and rolls down a window. "Need a ride?"

I close my cell. "Thanks, Kevin."

"Back to the farm?"

"Yeah."

He puts the truck in drive and we're on our way.

Sage grins at me. "Were you at the library?"

"No, I was at the Texas Historical Commission,

trying to find somebody to help me fix the chair in the shack."

Sage looks sad, and I wish I hadn't said anything. But she asks anyway.

"Well, what'd they say?"

"It was this dude named Mr. Adams. He said I need to bring him all kinds of proof that the shack is old and has some historical value, and I need to bring him pictures of it. He also said he wouldn't be able to do anything by Friday. I really wanted Grandma's chair fixed for the tour, Sage. He won't even come and look at it until sometime next week. So I guess that meeting was a bust."

The ride down the gravel road is a quiet one, until suddenly Sage goes off. "I've got it! I know what to do! Laura, I've got my camera in my backpack. Let me take some pictures of the shack and print them out. Then I'll do some research."

I'm confused but I go along with her. "Okay, then what?"

When Kevin stops the truck, Sage gets out. "Call that Mr. Adams guy back and tell him you need another meeting with him tomorrow after school."

"Why, Sage?"

She snaps a picture of the shack then keeps walking toward it. "Just do it and trust me. You know I've got your back."

Thursday morning I get up and shower while thinking about that chair. Sage said to make another appointment with Mr. Adams, and I did. I sure hope Sage has a plan. I'm still thinking about it on the bus.

Troy gets on and nods my way. "What's up, Dyson?"

"Hey, Troy."

I don't have time to be all sappy right now. Soon, Sage climbs on the bus and sits next to me. "Did you make the appointment?"

"Four thirty this afternoon. So what's the plan?"

She nods. "I'm going to ask for permission to leave early. Let's meet where my brother picked you up yesterday, okay? Oh! I almost forgot to tell you that I got special permission to go on the field trip with your class tomorrow! I'm taking pictures for the *Royal Crier*!"

"Awesome! I know you'll take great pictures."

She nods. "Of course I will."

I'm glad Sage is helping me, but I need Mr. Adams's help, too.

Twelve days ago, when my parents left me to live with Grandma, I felt like my life had gone from sugar to shame. And it had. The sugar was always here with Grandma and the other Lauras, but I was all caught up in a shame I brought with me.

All this time I called it a slave shack when it was really a family museum, waiting for me to see and understand everything. I can't end up being the worst Laura in the Line. Laura Ann may have broken her mother's heart, but at least she didn't break anything in the shack.

chapter twenty-nine

Right after school, I make my way to the Texas Historical Commission. Sage is standing at the front door. I forgot my baby powder this morning and I'm misting like crazy. I walk up to Sage. Neither of us smiles, but I notice she's got a paper sack in her hand.

"Is that a game changer?"

Sage shrugs. "I don't know. Let's go find out."

I open the door and we walk in. Mr. Adams sees us from his desk and waves. The little gate clicks, and Sage and I walk behind the counter. He shakes my hand.

"Hello again, Laura. And who is this you've brought with you?"

"This is my best friend, Sage Baxter."

Mr. Adams shakes her hand, too. "Let's go back to my desk."

We follow him, but even though he takes a seat, we keep standing. He opens up a file, and I see the map I drew for him. He looks back at us.

"Now, how can I help you, ladies?"

I look from Sage to Mr. Adams. "I'm not sure, but I think Sage has something for you. Right, Sage?"

Mist is now streaming down my back like creek water. Sage opens her paper sack and pulls out a binder. It's just like the one she made for the Pink Chips, except this one's blue, my favorite color. And it has my name on the front. But just as I reach for it, Sage puts it on Mr. Adams's desk.

"Laura told me you needed pictures of the shack and proof that it's been around for like, I don't know, forever."

He smiles. "Yes, among other things, I do need that information."

Sage continues and opens up the binder. The first picture is the one I saw her take yesterday. But when she turns the page, I'm mesmerized by the beauty she's shown in her pictures of the cemetery and the shack.

Mr. Adams and I examine them in silence, staring at the awesome shots Sage took. Then he turns the page, and there's a shot of the wall full of pictures.

What the what? She went inside? Without me? Without Grandma? I'm fighting the urge to blast her, because if it hadn't been for her climbing on Grandma's chair, we wouldn't be here in the first place. The shack doesn't have a welcome mat at the door. I take a few deep breaths and let them out slowly.

If she wasn't my best friend, and if I didn't know this was her way of trying to make things right, I'd call her out.

Sage points to a picture of Laura Elaine.

"She worked for the *Brooks County Tribune* and typed her articles on that typewriter sitting on the floor."

Mr. Adams is still looking. So am I. Sage reaches into her backpack and pulls out a newspaper.

"I spent the whole afternoon searching through microfilm at the *Tribune* and I found one of Laura Elaine's articles."

I'm staring at the article with Mr. Adams. I nudge Sage and give her a grin. Mr. Adams takes the article and examines it. Now it's my turn to add info.

"The typewriter in the shack has a broken G key. So when she typed that article, every *g* was handwritten."

I watch his eyes go from normal to wide. "Yes,

I probably wouldn't have noticed it if you hadn't told me."

Sage exhales. "There's your proof, Mr. Adams. But there's one more picture I want to show you."

Sage flips to a picture of the basket full of shattered wood.

"This used to be a very special chair, and I broke it."

I jump in. "It was an accident. I mean, seriously, I'm just as much to blame as she is."

Mr. Adams is busy checking off items on a list stapled to the inside of his file folder.

"Okay, ladies, thanks so much for the pictures and historical background. I'm going to put a big envelope of paperwork in the mail today and send it to Mrs. Anderson for her to fill out and send back. As soon as I get it, we'll be on our way to making the shack and the cemetery landmarks. Plus I'll send this picture of the wood pieces to Kim and Ana, two ladies I work with in furniture restoration. They'll let me know if they think the chair is restorable."

Sage and I stand there. I'm hoping Mr. Adams is not finished. It seems like he is when he stands and motions us to the door.

"I want to commend both of you on doing a wonderful job getting me the information I need to get the ball rolling. That was a lot of hard work."

I nod and so does Sage. When we get to the door, he shakes our hands again.

"It was so nice meeting both of you. Bye."

Sage and I say it together. "Bye."

Outside, Sage points across the street. "There's Kevin."

It's crazy quiet in the truck, but I don't want to talk right now. And I'm really thankful that Sage and Kevin seem to understand that. When we get to our mailbox, I ask Kevin to stop.

"Just let me out here. Thanks so much for the ride. I'll see you tomorrow, Sage."

"Okay. Are you really giving the tour tomorrow?"

I hold my chin in the air. "No matter what, I'm doing it."

They take off, and after getting the mail, I start my walk down the gravel road. I need it today, because I'm not sure if I'm going to cry or not. I don't want Grandma to see me crying. And this walk will give me time to get it all out before she sees me.

I take my time, looking at everything, hoping to think of some better ideas, but it doesn't work.

As I climb the hill, I see Troy. Again? This is the third day in a row. I shuffle over to him with my head tilted. He points to the house.

"Dad's just picking up a check."

"Oh." I put my backpack on the shack steps.

He pretends he's throwing a pitch. "Hey! I've been practicing that changeup. It's looking pretty good. But what about that knuckleball?"

I grin when I remember my promise. "Come on. Let's go to the mound."

That's just what I need right now. I need to throw. Troy's helping me, and he doesn't even know it. Hopefully, before we're through, this situation will make sense to me. And tomorrow, I'll be ready to give the best tour ever.

Grandma and Mr. Bailey come over to my pitching area. Troy's excited.

"Check out my new knuckleball, Dad."

He throws a perfect one, and Grandma speaks up.

"Fell out of the air like a dead bird."

Troy takes a bow and we all laugh. Then Grandma does something unexpected.

"Baby Girl, I've been talking with Mr. Bailey, and since tomorrow is a really big day for you, giving the tour and all, I thought we could celebrate by going to see the Astros play tomorrow night! I've got tickets for the four of us!"

My eyes widen. "Troy's going, too?"

She grins. "If he wants to, he can! I bought him a ticket!"

This is almost like a date! I'm waiting for Troy to say something smart so I can shove a ball in his mouth. But instead, he jumps at it.

"The Astros are playing the Yankees! That's going to be an awesome game. I am *so* there! Thanks, Mrs. Anderson. Yo, Dyson, you bringing a glove?"

"Ding."

Mr. Bailey laughs. "Troy and I will pick you two up tomorrow at six."

"We'll be ready!" I say that a little bit louder than I meant, but it's okay.

Sweet Mother of Milk Chocolate Hunky Chunkies! I'm going out on a date with Troy Bailey. That means I'll be with the finest boy in school, watching my most favorite sport ever.

As Troy and his dad leave, I hug Grandma. "I love you, but you've got to take your allergy medicine before we go. And no sneaking pork chop sandwiches into the ballpark, okay?"

Grandma holds up a finger. "And we won't have to leave early this time. Check out my new hat."

She reaches into her pocket, pulls out an Astros cap, and puts it on her head.

"How do I look?"

I hug her again. "Like a real baseball fan, Grandma."

chapter thirty

I'm up long before my alarm clock blares because I can't oversleep. Today wouldn't be a good time for that to happen. I've changed outfits three times and settle on a beautiful red and black dress that I usually wear to church. I braid and rebraid my hair because the part in the center of my head seems . . . off-center. I check my teeth. And my lip gloss. Everything has to be perfect.

I step out of my room and into the kitchen. Grandma wipes her hands on her apron and gives me the biggest grin I've seen in the two weeks I've been here.

"You look so beautiful, Laura Eboni."

I'm so used to her calling me Baby Girl that hearing my real name slide off her lips makes me feel grown-up and responsible for everything that happens today during the tour.

"I'm so nervous, Grandma."

"You're going to knock their socks off! And you've got a whole line of Lauras waiting to back you up. This is a big day for all of us. I'm so proud of you."

"Thanks, Grandma. I'm not very hungry this morning. I think it's stomach jitters."

"Got to eat something. Maybe just a little fruit."

I rush through my bowl of sliced apples and strawberries before grabbing my backpack and opening the door. The shack is the first thing I see. Instead of turning the other way, I want to run to it and hide all day. But I can't. It wouldn't be right. Today's a big day for the Line.

I've got black flats on to match my dress, but the crunch of the gravel under my feet makes me think of my nerves. I'm breathing in through my nose and out through my mouth, hoping to air out my stomach because the jitters are getting worse.

When the bus comes, our driver's smiling when the door opens. "Mornin'. You sure look nice this morning. Special day?"

"Uh-huh" is all I can say as I take a seat near the

middle of the bus. When Troy gets on, he slows down and stares at me.

"Why are you all dressed up?"

I turn and frown at him. "Because I'm giving the tour today and I don't want to look all busted."

He shrugs. "Well, you don't look busted."

"Thank you."

Did he just . . . ? My head makes an automatic left turn, and now I'm facing the back of the seat in front of me as my eyes open wider than the Mississippi River. I know my mouth's open, too, but I don't remember which muscles to use to shut it. I'm frozen, hopelessly numb dumb until he walks by and finds a seat. Maybe I'll wear this dress again on Monday.

Sunny gets on the bus and sashays by without speaking. Shane Doyles is right behind her. He slows down and is about to say something to me, but he doesn't. Instead, he stares at my outfit for a long time. Then he strolls away without saying a word. This dress must've told him to keep steppin'.

Sage is right behind him, and she makes a big deal out of my outfit too.

"You look runway ready, Laura."

I close my eyes. "Thanks, Sage. But between Troy basically telling me just five minutes ago that I look gorgeous and doing the tour this morning, I'm stressed to the max."

Sage pats my arm and whispers. "That explains why when I got on the bus, I could've sworn he was looking your way. He was . . . oh Laura, don't start misting."

I pull out a tissue and dab my face. "First I've got to ace this shack tour. Then I'm going to make that boy mine."

Sage giggles, and I do, too. She nudges me. "I've got to get my special camera equipment from my editor. Don't let the bus leave without me."

At eleven o'clock, I'm the first person in line, right in front of the doors to the field trip bus. My knees knock like clappers as my heart pounds so hard that I swear it's coming out. This will all be over in a few hours, but right now, that seems days away.

I peek over my shoulder at my classmates. Some are texting, while others are talking about what they think they may see in the shack. But I hear Sunny playing down the field trip to a crowd that includes Troy and London. Sage walks up to join them with her camera equipment, just in time to hear Sunny try to ruin everything.

"Don't get your hopes up that you're going to see something spectacular. It's not all that. Trust me. I've already been inside. Oh, and there's a cemetery, too. It's a little creepy, but mostly boring and ugly. Hope you brought something to read."

I turn back toward the front and stare at my reflection in the glass of the bus doors. Last week, Sunny's comments would've broken me down.

But not today.

I zone in on my eyes until I find my strike-out face. All the chatter, all the noise behind me fades to silence. I've seen baseball players smear black stuff under their eyes to fight the glare of the sun. If I had it, I'd wear it today, because I'm in a battle with the worst sun ever.

Sunny Rasmussen. And I'm going to sit her down.

Mrs. Jacobs raises a hand. "Okay, let's go. Remember, you're seventh graders, so act like it."

I take the first seat on the opposite side from the driver. Sage sits next to me and places her camera equipment between us on the floor. When Troy gets on, he sits right behind me. London sits across the aisle from him, but that changes when Sunny boards.

"What are you doing, London? I don't want to sit there. Come on."

London looks my way, then follows Sunny farther back.

The bus fills quickly, and soon we're on our way. Sage leans over and smoothes my hair.

"Are you okay?"

I nod without looking at her. "I just need to be quiet right now, okay?

She keeps talking. "I know you heard what Sunny said. But you've got to make the field trip fun, Laura. It's not all about Sunny. It's about how cool the shack is and all the awesomeness in the Laura Line. Don't let Sunny change that. Just be yourself."

Everything Sage said oozes through me and I know she's right, but my shoulders are so high and my jaw feels locked. I don't know if I can relax in time.

Soon the driver turns onto the gravel road and my stomach flips over and over again. Once he makes it up the hill and stops, I turn to Mrs. Jacobs.

"I need a minute, okay? Just . . . let me go in first and I'll be ready in a few."

Mrs. Jacobs smiles. "Okay. We'll wait."

I hop off the bus and rush to the shack. I climb the steps and open the door. Maybe I should've postponed until Mom and Dad could be here with me. They'd know what to say to calm me down.

It smells like a bakery inside. I look on the table and can't believe my eyes. There's a huge tray of chocolate chip cookies. Wait until Sunny Rasmussen sees this! But the more I look at those cookies, the more I realize this field trip isn't about proving Sunny Rasmussen *wrong*. It's about everything that's *right* inside me. It's proof that I'm not Fat Larda, but Laura, a descendant of the amazing Laura Line. And that's worth more than a stack of fresh-baked cookies.

I step back to the door and wave.

"Okay, I'm ready!"

I bring the tray of baked goodies outside and offer everyone a snack. The mood changes immediately. Sage takes pictures as my classmates, Mrs. Jacobs, and even the bus driver enjoy Grandma's homemade delights.

There's laughter and curiosity, and I notice a couple of guys trying to see what's out back. Troy's trying to give his own tour, but I give him a mean face and he stops. I ask Sage to whistle since she's good at it. All talking stops, and I begin.

"What you're about to see, inside and outside, are the coolest things ever. Let me just tell you first off, this is not a slave shack. It's more like a time capsule that never got buried. Yeah, that's what it's like! There's so much history in this place that I don't know where to begin."

The sound of tires crunching hard dirt and gravel makes everyone turn around. An old green and white van with the letters VW on the front makes its way toward us. The engine sounds funny, almost like a windup toy, and the van is shaped like a cucumber. When it stops and the door opens, just the sight of Mr. Adams brings a feeling I haven't felt since Mom left.

A feeling that everything is going to be okay.

But Mr. Adams represents something more than

just hope. Maybe he can fix what's broken. And I'm so happy that he thought enough of me to at least show up. He's out of breath when he reaches us.

"I postponed my early flight to Austin because I thought about this file all night. I just had to come. I'm pleased I made it in time."

I shake his hand. "I'm so glad you're here." I turn to my classmates. "Um, everybody, this is Mr. Bob Adams from the Texas Historical Commission. He's here to examine the shack and the cemetery, take pictures, whatever, to see if they can become landmarks."

There's a murmur going through the crowd, and I invite everyone inside. Mr. Adams is the last person and he checks his watch.

"My flight's changed to four, and my meeting in Austin's not until this evening, so I want to see everything before I go."

I step inside the shack. "Then we better get started."

As I talk, everybody listens. But when I grab the ledger, the shack goes creepy silent. I pretend the red fruit punch stains aren't on it, because right now, to me, it's the most perfect thing in the room.

"This is the ledger of the Laura Line. It has personal pictures, letters, awards, all kinds of things in it, about my ancestors. Some date back almost two hundred years. I'm going to put it on the table, but do not touch it. Don't even *ask* to touch it."

When I'm through, there's lots of talking as my classmates walk around to look at stuff. Mr. Adams uses his magnifying glass to examine pictures and Laura Jean's sewing machine. Occasionally he makes notes in a notepad that's similar to Sage's.

Troy raises his hand.

"Yes, Troy."

He points to the broken chair. "Why do you have this basket of firewood way over here if the fireplace is over there?"

What is he doing? He knows what happened. The memory of Monday night flashes through my mind quicker than a strike of lightning. I look around the room. Sunny folds her arms across her stomach. London's head lowers. Sage won't look at me. Troy's frowning at all of them.

And then I get it. Troy wants to shame the Pink Chips for what they did. And he's probably hoping I'll rat them out.

But instead I hold my head up. "It's not firewood. It's a chair."

Troy shoves his hands into his pockets. "Yeah, right. Why don't you tell everybody what happened."

His eyes shoot poison-tipped spears at Sunny

and London. I sigh and look directly at Sage. "What happened isn't important. You see firewood. I see something totally different. Let's just move on."

The room falls silent again, as most of my classmates have no idea what I'm talking about. Mr. Adams raises his hand and I call on him. He points to the typewriter.

"Laura, is this the typewriter you and Sage spoke of during our meeting?"

I grin at my girl before answering. "Sure is." I turn back to my classmates. "The letter G doesn't work. The typewriter belonged to Laura Elaine. She was a reporter for the *Brooks County Tribune*."

Sunny speaks without raising her hand.

"So how did she type for a newspaper without using the letter G?"

I'm about to answer when a voice speaks up from the back. "She wrote it in with an ink pen."

When did Grandma get here? I didn't see her come in! I smile and she smiles back.

There's another low murmur among my classmates. Sunny puts both hands on her hips and smirks. I'm praying something dumb comes out of her mouth. And she doesn't disappoint me when she stares at Grandma and asks, "How would you know that's what she did? I mean, seriously, were you there?"

Ding.

It's moments like this when I wish the shack had a concession stand. But instead, I'm content to stare at Sunny while Grandma rips her a new attitude.

"Yes, as a matter of fact, I was. Laura Elaine, the journalist, was my mother."

I hear someone from the back of the room say, "In your face, Sunny!"

Mr. Adams turns to Grandma as she points to the shattered wood in the corner.

"That used to be my special chair. I'd sit and watch my mother type, but she always kept a pen and a small bottle of ink next to her. I knew when she needed a *G* because she'd stop, let out the biggest sigh, then write it in. Her handwriting was so beautiful that you could hardly tell the difference between the typed letters and her handwritten *G*'s."

"You actually watched her do that?" asks Mr. Adams.

Grandma nods. "Sometimes well past my bedtime."

He grins. "That's an amazing story."

I interrupt. "I've got one more thing to show you in here. And it's mega."

I tell everyone about Laura Mae's letter and what it said about the first Laura. Some of my classmates check out the wall of pictures looking for her. Others have that look on their faces that I had on mine when I first read the letter.

Sunny can't believe it.

"Are you trying to say that the first Laura in your . . . line sacrificed her freedom for those four kids we've been reading about in history class? You expect us to believe that?"

Troy steps forward. "I do."

Sage nods. "Me, too."

I press the ledger against me and walk to the wall.

"Everybody gather in and stare at this wall of pictures. Now, very slowly, start walking backward, but keep your eyes on the wall."

They're doing it and nobody's asking why. So I get ready to show them what I've seen.

"If you look closely, you'll see . . ."

London points. "It's a face. I see it! Right there! The pictures outline the side of a face!"

Grandma stands beside me as I reveal the biggest news ever. "You're right, London. It's the profile of the first Laura. Remember the handout Mrs. Jacobs gave to us two weeks ago? This is what her sketch would've looked like if she had been included."

It gets so loud in the shack that I can barely understand what's going on. I look over at the picture profile and get teary eyed all over again.

Troy's trying to ease closer to the pictures. "What else do you know about her?"

I shrug. "I don't know her story, but I'm sure my

grandma does, and one day she'll tell me. See, some things were meant to be put in the ledger, but other things are for conversation between one Laura and another. Right, Grandma?"

She puts her arm around me. "Exactly."

I raise my hand and point my thumb toward the backyard.

"I've got something else to show you. Let's go outside."

Everyone crowds around the cemetery as I introduce each Laura and the highlights of her life according to the ledger. I take my time, giving each one her fair share of the spotlight. Sage takes pictures of each cross, and Mr. Adams makes notes as I speak.

When I'm finished, I say, "Well, that's the end of the tour. Any questions?"

Of all the hands to go up, I never expected Troy's to be the first. I point to him.

"When you die, do you want to be buried back here with the other Lauras?"

I don't hesitate. "No doubt. I'm part of the Laura Line. It's where I belong."

It's quiet now, which to me is normal for a graveyard. But Mr. Adams begins to clap, and others clap with him. As I take a bow, Mr. Adams goes back into the shack.

After my classmates head to the bus, Sage and I

rush to the window to see what Mr. Adams is doing in the shack. He's on his cell phone, bending over the basket of wood, picking up the pieces and examining them. When he spots us looking at him through the window, he smiles, ends his call, and comes out of the shack.

He shakes my hand. "That was a marvelous presentation! I'm so glad I came to hear it."

I can't help but grin. "Thanks, Mr. Adams. So did you find out anything about the chair?"

His smile vanishes. "I just had a conversation with Kim and Ana from Furniture Restoration. I'm afraid I've got bad news for you."

My heart sinks. "What?"

"Kim, Ana, and I agree. It's not fixable, Laura. I'm so sorry."

It's as if I just got three scoops of my favorite ice cream and dropped them in the dirt.

Sage takes a few steps backward. I lock eyes with him.

"You're sure?"

Sage's face reddens as Mr. Adams nods. I stare at the ground because my next look will be at Grandma. And I need a minute to prepare myself before seeing her face. I push dirt with the toe of my shoe, trying to busy my mind with something else besides the need to cry.

Finally, my eyes meet hers. She's trying to hold a smile, but it keeps fading. She whispers to me, "It's okay, Baby Girl. And I'm excited about that baseball game!"

But it's far from okay.

Sage drags to the bus with lots of pain in her walk. Even from the back I can tell she's crying. I turn to Grandma, not sure what to say, so I rush to the bus, leaving her, Mrs. Jacobs, and Mr. Adams standing at the shack. They can't see me cry.

I'm the last student to board the bus, and all eyes are on me. Sunny's sitting next to London, and when she looks my way, she shouts, "Hey, Fat Larda, what's it like owning a slave shack? How embarrassing."

A few classmates giggle, and I scan the faces staring at me. Sunny starts up again.

"Answer me, Larda. What's it like . . ."

A surge of anger flows through me, and I'm ready to fight until a holler stops me.

"Shut up, Sunny!"

Heads turn. Students gasp. And I almost fall in the aisle when London stands and points her finger in Sunny's face.

"I got chill bumps in that shack. You're the one who should be embarrassed for not figuring out that it's the most incredible piece of history ever! Do you have anything like that at your house to celebrate *your* ancestors? Oh, wait. I can answer that. *No!* Laura's got almost two hundred years of history right over there, and she let us see it. And I hope she invites me again."

London moves to the back and sits with Sage. The bus is still quiet, and I'm not sure what to do. All heads turn back to me. Even Troy looks my way. Everyone's staring at me, and I'm beginning to mist. It's time for me to find a seat in the back with Sage and London.

As I move down the aisle, some kids continue to giggle, while others just stare at me. I hold my head up, Laura Line style, and walk to the back. Someone's moving behind me. I turn to see Troy heading to the back, too. I take the seat in front of Sage and London. Troy takes the seat on the other side of the aisle from me and asks the first question.

"So when your grandma tells you about the first Laura, are you going to tell us?"

I shrug. "Sure, why not."

Troy grins and shakes his head. I turn to Sage, who's wiping her face.

"And, uh, Sage took awesome pictures and brought them to Mr. Adams's office. That's why he came. I'm sure of it. And now he's going to help my grandma preserve the rest of the stuff in the shack. So Sage gets a bunch of credit, too."

London nudges Sage. "You helped Laura get that guy to come out here to see the shack?"

Sage shrugs. "It's the least I could do."

London looks over at me. "Now that's a real friend."

I agree. "Yeah. My BFF."

I'm through with this conversation because I've got a hot date tonight, and that superfine Hunky Chunky is sitting right across from me. And he just took up for me like a Hunky Chunky should.

Maybe tonight, at the game, we'll get to know each other even better. And when they play "The Star-Spangled Banner" and the fireworks light up the night, he'll hang a kiss on me bigger than the rockets' red glare or bombs bursting in air.

Tonight, I'm wearing extra lip gloss.

chapter thirty-one

I've got my classic Astros jersey on again with my Levi's and orange Sketchers. I stare at my last two Almond Joys sitting in that big bag alone. Well, this is a special occasion, so I'm eating one. I take my time, enjoying that chocolate and coconut. But when it's gone, I look at the lone one in the bag. Maybe I'll take that one home with me.

I'm putting lip gloss on when the telephone rings. Grandma shouts to me.

"I've got it!"

But I grab the telephone receiver off the wall and put it to my ear. "Hello?"

"Hey, Dyson, it's me, Troy. My dad and I aren't going to make it tonight. Sorry."

"What? Why not?"

"Dad won the bid on a huge job, and we're on our way to get started on it right now. This is big-time for Bailey and Bailey. And Dad always tells me businessmen have to handle business before pleasure. I'll see you tomorrow when we come and cut the grass. Tell Mrs. Anderson we'll pay her back for the tickets. Bye."

Click.

I'm in the kitchen, holding a dead phone, wondering why I ever liked Troy Bailey. He's lying about that big job. I know why he's not coming. He doesn't want to be seen with me.

And to think I taught him my best pitches. I listened to his family drama. I even went inside the shack so we'd have something to talk about. I thought he was beginning to like me.

And then, when he complimented my dress today, I just knew . . .

I hang up the receiver and take a seat at the table. Grandma stands in the archway of the kitchen with her Astros hat on. I break the news.

"It was Troy. They're not coming."

Grandma puts her arm around me. "I know you're disappointed, but it's going to be okay. I'm sure they had a good reason. We'll still have a great time. Are you ready?"

"I'm ready."

Grandma's talking about the starting pitchers and who she thinks will win. I'm half listening to her because I'm so mad at Troy that I can't concentrate. She keeps talking.

"And this time, I brought money for our snacks. No pork chop sandwiches."

"Okay."

Grandma gets a good parking spot, and soon we're in our seats watching the game. She's shouting stuff that I usually shout, but tonight I'm just not into it. I glance at the empty seat next to me. "The Star-Spangled Banner" comes and goes with fireworks in the air but none for my lips. Wait until I see him tomorrow. After I finish going to the left on him, he may not ever speak to me again.

Grandma stays awake for the whole game. She even buys one of those big foam fingers with WE'RE NUMBER ONE! written across it. All the way to the car she talks about how great the Astros did in their win over the Yankees. Occasionally I try to add something to the conversation, but I just want this night to be over.

When she turns onto the gravel road, the conversation changes.

"Baby Girl, I can tell you didn't enjoy yourself."

I force myself to perk up. "Yes, I did, Grandma. And thanks for getting the tickets."

She keeps driving. "There's a reason for everything. You need to remember that, okay?"

I don't say anything, because Troy had a rotten reason—and I didn't like it.

I go to my room and take off my jersey to get ready for bed. Tomorrow my parents will be here, and I can't wait to see them. Maybe I'll get up early and go throw, just to get this sadness off me before I see them. There's no way I'll let Troy ruin that, too.

Early Saturday morning my cell buzzes. I tap Answer.

"Hello?"

"Hey! It's Dad! How are you?"

Sleep leaves me, and I turn my body to sit on the side of the bed.

"Dad! It's about time you guys called me! When are you coming home? I've got so much to tell you. Guess what! Grandma and I went to an Astros game last night. She got tickets! You wouldn't believe how much she knows about the game. And I went into the shack and—"

"Whoa! Slow down! It sounds like you've been very busy. Save some of that conversation for me and your mom when we get there. We're about two hours away!"

"What?"

"Yep, we wanted to surprise you, so we waited until we couldn't anymore. We'll see you in a couple of hours. Hold on, your mom wants to talk to you."

"Baby Girl?"

"Hi, Mom! I'm so excited! Guess what? I went in the shack."

Silence. Then:

"I can't even tell you how happy I am, Laura Eboni. I know your grandma is, too."

I get up and walk as I talk. "She is. So you'll be here in a couple of hours?"

Mom giggles. "In a couple of hours."

I bite my lip, thinking about everything that's happened since she's been gone.

"I can't wait to see you."

"I can't wait to see you, too, and hear about all the things you did while we were gone. I love you. See you soon."

I end the call, bubbling inside, knowing my parents aren't far away. But another part of me hurts. I got dumped on my first date. We were so close to making it happen. I can't believe Troy Bailey . . . bailed on me.

I reach into the drawer and pull out a pair of old sweats and clip my iPod to my pants. On my way through the kitchen, Grandma offers me breakfast. I rush over and hug her.

"Mom and Dad are on their way! They're two hours from here."

"Hot diggitty dog! I'll put more biscuits in the oven and fry up more bacon!"

I drink a glass of orange juice and take a bite of toast. "I'm going to throw before Mom and Dad get here."

Grandma gives me a thumbs-up. "Sounds like a plan."

I push the screen door open and walk toward my pitching area. Dad said to throw until everything makes sense. How long am I going to be out here? All day?

Once I get my earbuds in and turn the music up, I grab a ball, split my pointer and middle fingers away from each other, and grip that thing like crazy. With everything I've got, I hurl a heater at the target as I think about how Troy canceled on me last night.

POP!

After all I've done for him. Seriously, the only good pitches that boy has are the ones I taught him. I pick up a ball and throw another heater.

BLAM!

I even listened to his sob story about wanting to spend time with his dad. I felt sorry for him and tried to make him smile when he didn't have anything to smile about.

BLAM!

Fastball after fastball bangs the target until my arm feels like cooked spaghetti. There were at least twenty baseballs in that bucket. Now it's empty.

I lean against a thick oak tree as my shoulder throbs from hurling fastballs. Catching my breath is another issue. I threw too fast. But I couldn't help it. I shuffle over to the tree and put the baseballs back in the bucket.

There's a tap on my shoulder, and I almost throw an elbow because the first thing that pops into my mind is a snake dangling from a tree.

"Whoa, you almost hit me, Dyson!"

I turn around. It *was* a snake. A low-down, dirty one. He's grinning, showing those dimples. I take my earbuds out as he grabs a ball from my bucket.

"How was the game last night?"

Right now, I think his dimples are upside-down pimples. "You'd know if you had been there."

He tosses the ball in the air and catches it. "Yeah, uh, couldn't help it. But Dad locked up that new contract last night. We've got another lawn gig. Hey, you got a minute?"

Why should I give him a minute? He couldn't find one for *me* last night. Unless he had a hundred acres to cut, he could've made the game before we finished singing the national anthem. Where was he during the rockets' red glare and bombs bursting in air?

His head tilts. "What's wrong with you, Dyson?"

I unload. "If you're too embarrassed to be seen with me, Troy, then just say so. You don't have to go around acting one way with me when you're here and then a totally different way when we're at school."

He frowns. "What are you talking about?"

I'm trying not to cry, so I just clam up. "Nothing. Forget it."

Now he's staring at me.

"We had a new client, Dyson. And then Dad and I were busy last night working on something. We worked until midnight, but we got it done."

I roll my eyes. "Good for you."

He steps closer. "No, Dyson. Good for you. Here, take this."

He hands me a flyer.

PERSONAL TRYOUT INVITATION

We are excited to offer you
an opportunity to try out for the first
BROOKS COUNTY SELECT BASEBALL TEAM.
Tryouts will be held on **Saturday, April 25th**
from **10:00 a.m. to 2:00 p.m.**
Please be prepared to pitch, hit, and catch. After

tryouts the coaches will make up a roster, contact the players who made the team, and send out a practice schedule.

We look forward to seeing you at tryouts.

Sincerely,

John Bailey, Coach

I read it twice and still want an explanation.

"What is this, Troy?"

He sighs. "Haven't you ever seen a flyer for baseball tryouts?"

I'm still confused. "Yeah, but why are you giving me one?"

"Quit playin', Dyson. Your pitches are filthy! You've got to play on our team."

I shake my head. "A girl on an all-guys team? I'll get clowned. It'll be pure torture."

He pulls another flyer from his pocket. "But you're a ballplayer, Dyson. And a good one! This is what Dad and I were doing last night after the new job. And not everybody's getting one of these. Only the good players. You're the first person, well, after me, who got an invitation. So are you going to try out or what?"

I put my glove on my hip. "Dang, I just got it! Now you're rushing me for a decision? I mean, I can already hear people making fun of me."

Troy spits in the dirt. "Seriously? I know guys who

would give their right arm to get their paws on one of these flyers."

I look him in the eye. "But I'm not a guy, and I don't have paws."

He turns away from me, points to the cemetery, then glares me down.

"You're not a guy, but you're a descendant of Laura Ann. What about all that bragging you were doing the other day? Now's your chance to back it up. I can't believe you'd quit before you even tried. Anyway, I've got grass to cut."

He walks away, and I'm left holding the flyer like it's sacred. I've never had the opportunity to try out for a real team. What will Dad say?

I go back to my pitching area and sit on my mound, staring at the invitation. I turn it over, hold it up to the light, and even smell it. It's legit.

Suddenly, a horn honks from the bottom of the hill. They're here.

chapter thirty-two

I fold the flyer and stuff it into my pocket and rush toward the house. Dad barely makes it out of the car before I wrap my arms around his waist. He grabs my arms and twirls me until my legs leave the ground.

"Stop, Dad, you're making me dizzy!"

We both laugh, but he keeps holding on to me.

"Look at you! Something's different. Have you grown? You look even prettier than you did before I left. That must be it!"

I give him a shy smile because I have grown, but it has nothing to do with my height. Mom stands and looks over the roof of the car. We're eye to eye, and

I'm careful not to reveal anything. She's got a black belt in Eye-ish.

"Oh, Laura, come here!"

Gravel scatters beneath my feet as I rush to feel her arms around me. She smells like home.

"Mom, I missed you so much."

Grandma waits patiently for her hugs and gets them from both Mom and Dad. She opens the screen door.

"Y'all come on in. I've got brunch ready."

There's a feast on the table and it all smells good. Mom and Dad take off their military hats and wait for me to wash my hands before coming back to the table. I sit between them as we dig into Grandma's good cooking.

Dad leans back in his chair. "So how did things go?"

I scoot fruit from one side of my plate to the other, waiting for Grandma to spill her guts and get me in big-time trouble for what I did. But instead, she lifts me up with what she says.

"Today is one of the saddest days of my life. I've enjoyed having Laura Eboni here with me so much that I don't know what I'm going to do when she's not here."

Mom reaches over and hugs me. Dad puts his arms around my shoulders and chuckles.

"See, I knew you'd be okay."

I scoot back from the table. "I'm finished. I think I'll take a walk."

Dad nods as he chews. "Have you been throwing?"

I nod. "Like crazy."

I step outside and walk toward the shack. Pain streaks across my chest as I realize this time tomorrow I'll be on my way home. I won't be able to just walk over here and hang out whenever I want.

But it's not so much the shack I'll miss, and that's why I keep walking. As I make my way to the backyard, to the cemetery, I stand in front of the crosses and think of each Laura. I don't want to leave them. They've helped me figure out so much stuff about myself.

But there's one thing I need to give to them. I've been putting it off because I didn't know how. Now I'm running out of time and I've got to say this. So I stand in front of Laura Ann's cross, where I feel the most comfortable, and say what's on my mind.

"I broke the chair. I don't think anybody except Lauras should be responsible for what goes on in that shack. I know each of you was in there at one time or another. And you took care of it. But I made a big mistake, and I want to say I'm so sorry."

I know they weren't perfect. It's clear to me from the pictures that they were overweight, but happy with themselves. And their letters proved they struggled with all kinds of different stuff but never gave up. Through everything, the Line stayed strong.

So I keep talking.

"Thanks to you, for the first time since third grade, I'm not Fat Larda. I'm proud to be part of the Line, and I'll do everything I can to represent it."

I stuff my hand into my pocket and rub the flyer.

"Laura?"

It's Mom. Grandma's with her. They stand next to me and take my hands. We stand in silence, staring at the crosses. All three of us know the stories. And we know the Lauras.

But as I stand there with Mom and Grandma, it dawns on me that at this very moment, I'm with my very own Laura Line, the living one. They've both followed the paths they wanted to take. And it didn't matter what people thought or said about them.

After a few moments, I break the silence.

"So let's go inside, all three of us at the same time."

Mom's head tilts. "You really went inside?"

I giggle. "More than once. Come on!"

Mom nods as Grandma wipes a tear away. We walk hand in hand to the shack before letting go and making our way up the steps. Once Mom comes in, she looks at the table.

"Where's the little chair?"

It's time I come clean. But just before I speak up, Grandma does.

"It broke by accident."

I pull out a chair for Grandma and nod at the other seat. "You can have that one, Mom. I don't need to sit right now. But I need to hear the truth about something."

I've got Mom's and Grandma's full attention as I walk to the window and stop. I'm biting my lip to cut any extra drama that might try to drip out, because this has been bothering me for a few days. So I slowly turn back to Grandma and ask what I need to know.

"What can you tell me about the first Laura?"

Grandma reaches for the ledger and holds it close to her heart as she stands and moves to a rocking chair. Then she turns and looks into me, like she did at Mrs. Jacobs's house.

"I can tell you what's been told to me. Come close."

Mom's not moving, as if she's giving Grandma center stage. Maybe this is between Grandma and me, but I need to know what really happened. So I sit on the floor at Grandma's feet and look up into her face as she begins a gentle rock in the chair.

"I'm ready, Grandma."

Grandma gets that spacey look on her face as she blinks slowly and begins.

"First, her name was Zahara, not Laura. She was a beautiful girl, with skin as smooth as silk fabric. She had the cutest little nose and lovely, full lips. Zahara lived in Mendeland, Africa, with her mother, father, and younger sister, Kinzi. It's no longer called Mendeland. It's now known as Sierra Leone."

I cross my legs. "Did Zahara like her little sister?"

Grandma looks down at me and smiles. "Oh, yes. Zahara liked to play hiding games with Kinzi. But one day, as they played, Zahara was captured, shackled, and forced to board a ship loaded with others who'd been treated the same horrible way. She had never been on a ship before, and the movement across the ocean made her very sick. Many days and nights later, when the ship stopped moving, Zahara believed she had been brought back home to Mendeland."

I shake my head. Grandma reaches down and rubs my shoulder as she continues.

"Scared, sick, and starving, Zahara ended up in a land she'd never seen. It was Cuba. There, she and the other captives were sold to two Spanish men. Those two Spaniards transferred Zahara and the other captives to a smaller ship called the *Amistad*. Since Zahara was only fifteen, she was placed in the back on the bottom deck of the schooner, with four other children. Are you getting this, Laura Eboni?"

I'm not sure I'll be able to handle it. I've got a tear backup forming and Grandma just started the story.

"I think so."

She continues. "Now back on the water and feeling sick again, Zahara begged for someone to help her, pleading that a mistake had been made and that she needed to get back home to help take care of her sister. It was then that she overheard two captives planning a revolt. They whispered until everybody knew the plan. Zahara had never killed anyone, but she knew a takeover was the only way she could get back home to her family."

I put my hand on the arm of Grandma's rocker. "I bet she was scared."

Grandma nods and keeps going. "As the battle began, Zahara was told to stay with the four little ones huddled in the very back, named Kali, Teme, Kagne, and Margru. Zahara comforted the children, like she did her sister back home. She stayed with the children after the captives took over the ship and believed they were heading back home to Mendeland, but at night, as the captives slept, the Spaniards actually steered the ship away from Africa. The *Amistad* ended up in Connecticut."

I frown. "What a dirty rotten trick."

Grandma keeps rocking. "Yes, it was. So Zahara

kept her promise to the children and took care of them, even as the American guards forced them into a small jail."

I'm ready to cry again. "What happened?"

Grandma motions me to sit in the rocker next to her. I do and wait patiently for her to finish the story. She begins to rock again, but now, she's looking out the window.

"One night, Zahara heard a conversation between one of the jail guards and a man dressed in all black with black boots and a black hat. This man in black pulled paper and coins from his pocket and gave them to the guard, who stuffed the paper and coins into his pocket."

I start rocking in my chair. "This doesn't sound good, Grandma."

"It's not. The man in black pointed to the children, and the guard opened the jail and tried to shackle them, but Zahara pushed him away. Others awakened from the noise, but they were warned to stay back. Zahara kept fighting, even though the guard hit her with his fist. Then suddenly, the man in black whistled. The guard turned and saw the man was now pointing at Zahara instead of the children, so he stopped fighting her, opened the jail, and left.

"So the man in black left the children alone?"

"Yes. And Zahara believed she'd won the battle

and the fight was over."

My knower stirs. "But it wasn't."

Grandma lowers her eyes and shakes her head. "When the guard came back, instead of clamping the cold iron chains around the children, he shackled Zahara's hands, feet, and neck. It was then that she realized the man in black was taking her instead of the children. And since her job was to protect the children, she chose not to fight."

I grab my pigtails. "Grandma, I don't know if I can—"

"You can, Baby Girl. It's almost over."

I can't stop the tears, and maybe I'm not supposed to. So I keep listening.

"The children cried, but Zahara told them to be strong. Then, as if she knew, she said to the children: 'Promise me that when you return to Mendeland, you'll find my family and tell them I love them. And tell my sister, Kinzi, I will be back to play with her soon.' And the children promised."

I'm wiping my eyes. "Why didn't the other captives help her?"

Grandma's wiping hers, too. "I don't know. All I was told by my grandmother, Laura Jean, was the guard pushed her and made her leave the jail cell. As she walked away in shackles, Zahara watched the guard grab a paper and a stick with paint at the end."

I'm confused. "A stick with paint at the end? I don't understand."

Grandma nods. "We think she was describing a pen."

I shrug. "Oh. What did he do with the pen and paper?"

Grandma closes her eyes. "We believe the guard had a checklist of every person aboard the *Amistad* on that paper. We also think the night Zahara was sold to the man dressed in black, the guard scribbled through Zahara's name as if she'd never existed. To prove our point, in all of the historic documents discussing the *Amistad* and its captives, there is never a mention of a young girl from Mendeland named Zahara."

I'm ready to fight. "But the other captives knew! They knew about Zahara! Why didn't they try to find her once they were freed?"

"Maybe they did. But her name had changed from Zahara to Laura. How would they find her?"

I glance over at Mom. She's hurting. I see it in her face. I see it in Grandma's. All three of us sit in silence, and I believe we're feeling the same pain. And the only thing I can think of that would connect our emotions like that would be our knowers. Maybe we're connected all the way down the Line. That's why each of the Lauras felt so close to me. It's because they were.

I'm shaking my head because it's so hard to believe.

So I tell Grandma how I'm feeling.

"Do you think anybody would ever believe that story, Grandma? I mean, there's nothing to prove it's true."

We sit for a moment as my question lingers in the air. Finally Grandma says what I should already know.

"Does it matter what others think? For us, as members of the Laura Line, to deny her existence means we deny ours. If we ignore her again, then we're no different from the men who kidnapped and sold her into slavery. They made sure there was no record of her. They wanted to erase the fact of her existence. I refuse to do that to her again."

Silence hovers in the room long enough for me to understand the importance of what Grandma's saying. And as if Mom knew, she calls me on it.

"Laura, before I left for Killeen, I asked you a question, but you didn't have an answer. I told you I wanted one when I got back. So here we are, and I'll ask you again. Who are you?"

I turn toward the pictures on the wall, then stand and raise my chin toward the silhouette of the first Laura. Grandma stands next to me and raises her chin, too. Mom joins us before I tell her what I couldn't two weeks ago.

"I'm Laura Eboni Dyson, the youngest member of the Laura Line, and I can do anything."

The paper in my pocket digs at me, so I take it out and look at it. Then I take the ledger from Grandma's hand and lead her back to the table. Once I put the ledger on the table and Grandma takes a seat, I let out a big sigh.

"Mom, Grandma, there's something I want to do. I got an invitation to try out for a baseball team. I'm scared. I mean, I've always dreamed of playing baseball, and now I've got a shot at making that dream come true."

Mom and Grandma wait patiently for me to finish. But instead of telling them about it, I show them.

I grab the ledger and put it on the table between us. I open the ledger and turn the pages until I get to the back, where there's extra cover sheets and plastic sheet protectors. I take one of each out of the ledger and place them on the table.

As Mom and Grandma watch, I put the flyer in the plastic sheet protector and insert it in the front of the ledger. Grandma covers her mouth and so does Mom. I put a cover sheet over it and then look up.

"It doesn't matter if I make the team. What matters is that I don't pass up the opportunity to try."

chapter thirty-three

There's a knock on the shack door, and I open it. It's Dad. He looks over at Grandma.

"The guys are finished cutting the grass."

Grandma gets up. "I'm on my way." She turns to us and winks. "We'll have plenty of opportunities to finish these stories."

Mom and I follow Grandma out of the shack. The bright sun shines on my face, and I feel incredible. Now I want everybody to know about the Laura Line and the shack. I want the world to know about the exceptional women in my family. And I can start by acting like one of them.

I reach for Dad's hand. "I'd like to introduce you to a boy who goes to my school, and his dad."

When we're close enough, I do the honors.

"This is Troy. We have history class together and he pitches for our school's team. And that's his dad."

Mr. Bailey sticks out his hand. "John Bailey."

Dad shakes his hand. "Larry Dyson. Nice to meet you."

Mr. Bailey says, "So you taught Laura how to pitch?"

Dad grins. "I sure did. Have you seen her curveball?"

Mr. Bailey chuckles. "Not only did I see it, she taught Troy how to throw it!"

They laugh, and Troy holds up his hand for me to give him a high-five. I give him a hard slap. He checks his hand for red marks. I did that on purpose. I'm still mad because he bailed on me last night and I missed out on my "rockets' red glare" kiss, even though it looks like the "new client" excuse is legit.

Mr. Bailey nudges Troy.

"Did you give Laura the flyer?"

"Yes, sir."

Dad looks my way. "What flyer?"

I swallow to clear my throat before giving him the good news.

"I'm going to try out for Mr. Bailey's select baseball team."

Dad's face lights up. "Baseball? Are you serious?"

Troy starts to hold up his hand for another high five but changes his mind. Instead, he just smiles, and those deep dimples call for me to come take a ride. I can't stop the sudden daydream since I'm already picturing myself at a baseball stadium, waving at the crowd from inside Troy's dimple as he carries me out to the pitcher's mound. Then his voice brings me back to the present.

"Glad you're going to try out, Dyson. We may go undefeated!"

I smile. "Heck to the double yes we will!"

Mr. Bailey steps closer to Dad. "Laura's tryout is basically a formality. I already see her in my starting rotation of pitchers. Listen, would you be interested in helping me coach the team? Laura tells me you played ball in college."

Dad's pumped. "I was the starting catcher. Hit pretty good, too. I'd love to help out."

Mr. Bailey reaches in his pocket and gives Dad a card. "Perfect. Let's get together for lunch early next week. I've got a few ideas and I'd like to hear yours, okay?"

Dad takes the card and shakes Mr. Bailey's hand. "You bet. I'm looking forward to it, John."

Later that evening, after Grandma, Mom, and Dad have all gone to bed, I stand in my room and stare at the shack from my window. I can't believe I'm getting all sentimental about this. I'm going to ding myself for it. But I can't help how I'm feeling.

Why did that chair have to break? I hate being part of the reason why it's broken. And now I'll have to look at that basket of busted wood the rest of my life. I'll probably end up writing about it in the ledger.

Since this is my last night, I think I'll take a flashlight and go out there, just to say my good-byes. I wrap my robe around me and scoot into my slippers. I get the flashlight, open the dresser, and grab my last Almond Joy. I'm not taking it home. I'm taking it now. I tiptoe out of the house and across the yard.

I think about what Grandma told me she did when she was a child, sneaking inside the shack so she could spend time with her mom. It all makes sense to me now.

Once I get to the door, I turn the doorknob, go in, and walk straight to the ledger. I want to apologize again for the chair, but suddenly, a calm rushes over me. I close my eyes, take a deep breath, and let it out. I feel better than I ever have about what happened.

Maybe what I'm feeling is the Line forgiving me. I find a rocking chair, take a seat, and unwrap my last piece of chocolate as I enjoy this last night in the quiet of the shack.

I'm all packed on Sunday morning. I've folded my clothes neatly—unlike how they were when I came here—and my luggage is stacked and ready to go.

As I make my way to the car, I can't believe how emotional I am. And it gets worse when I find Grandma waiting for me at the car. I'm not sure how long we hug, but it feels the same way Mom's hug felt when she left for Killeen two weeks ago. I pull away and look at Grandma.

"So can I come back on Saturday?"

Grandma lets out a hearty laugh. "I can't wait! Maybe there will be a good baseball game on for us to watch."

I shake my head. "Grandma, what are you going to do when baseball season is over?"

Her eyebrows scrunch together. "When does the season end?"

I grin. "The World Series happens in October. After that, there's no more baseball until spring."

Grandma claps her hands. "Oh, that's perfect! It'll end just in time for basketball season. Edna and I have season tickets to the Houston Rockets!"

I giggle. "Grandma! You're a major sports fan! Maybe Saturdays can be *our* day."

She winks. "How about we have an early Saturday morning brunch date twice a month, around the time when Bailey and Bailey cut my grass?"

My eyes widen. "Ooooh, yeah! That sounds awesome, Grandma!"

"Then Saturday brunch it is, starting next Saturday! I love you."

I hug her and get into the car. "Love you, too, Grandma."

I wave through the back window until Dad turns onto the gravel road. Then he starts talking about baseball and all his ideas for the team.

Mom reaches for my hand, and I give it to her. "Are you okay?"

I nod and smile. "Heck to the double yeah. I'm better than ever."

acknowledgments

I'd like to thank my Lord and Savior, Jesus Christ, for everything and everybody in my life. My family has been so supportive, especially my guys, Reggie, Phillip, and Joshua. Everything I do, I have you in mind because I love you.

Thank you, Frank Morrison, for *The Laura Line*'s amazing cover.

Thank you, Trish Lowery, for doing early edits on *The Laura Line*. And, thank you, Rebecca Springer, Pat Baker, and Barbara Scott for the final ones. A special thanks goes to Juliet White, Tim Kane, and Petula Workman, my critique partners, for reading through all five thousand versions of this story. ☺

Thank you, Christine Taylor-Butler, Neal Shusterman, and Donna Gephart, for your unfailing support. Thanks to all the writers, editors, and friends who encouraged me.

I'll give props to the 2010–2011 sixth and seventh

graders of Bobby Shaw Middle School in Pasadena, Texas; Quail Valley Middle School in Sugar Land, Texas; and Sartartia Middle School in Sugar Land, Texas, for their awesome story ideas!

Thanks to Bob Brinkman, Kim Barker, and Ana Clark, three incredible specialists from the Texas Historic Commission. Thank you for sharing your knowledge.

I will forever be grateful to my editors, Kristin Daly Rens and Sara Sargent, and my agent, Jennifer Rofé. Thank you for surrounding me with understanding and patience. Thanks for helping me find and keep Laura's voice throughout her story, so that she could resolve her issues her way. I believe the four of us have formed our own "Line," and I'm proud to be a part of it.